"We usually watch the Christn side looking in, as we see Ma... ...ph, the shepherds, and then the wise men all arrive in Bethlehem. But what would it have looked like to be on the inside? Katy Morgan's *The Promise and the Light* helps young readers imagine what it might have felt like for Mary and Joseph. And it leaves us hoping there will be a sequel describing what happened next!"

SINCLAIR FERGUSON, Author,
The Dawn of Redeeming Grace

"Fed up with school nativities and sentimental Christmas cards? Then *The Promise and the Light* is for you. It's a fantastic retelling of the Christmas story from the perspective of those who witnessed it first-hand. It's historically informed and beautifully reimagined. The result is an engrossing tale through which the message of Jesus shines."

TIM CHESTER, Crosslands Training;
Author, *Enjoying God*

"Employing the voices of Mary, Joseph and Zechariah, Katy Morgan creates a lovely personal retelling of the Christmas narrative, carefully evoking the time and the place, and tying all that happens into God's big story. Wonderful!"

BOB HARTMAN, Bestselling Author

"As the mom of young readers, I'm always looking for books that stir their imagination while also pointing them to the Scriptures. This is such a book! *The Promise and the Light* is a wonderful retelling of the Christmas story through the eyes of the biblical characters. If you're looking for a family read-aloud this Christmas, or for a book for your kids to read for themselves, this book captures the wonder of Christmas while retaining the power of the biblical narrative."

COURTNEY REISSIG, Managing Director,
Risen Motherhood

"I can't wait to read this book aloud with my kids this Advent. As a dad, I love the engaging narrative, alternating perspectives, and fleshing-out of Christmas truths to provoke curiosity. As a pastor, I love the notes in the back that give the bones of biblical truth and historical facts that give substance to the project. How critical, in a world of fairy tales, with many good ones on our shelves, that we drive home for our kids that *this* story is not make-believe. Katy unveils the truth and beauty of Christmas—both for our kids and for their parents."

DAVID MATHIS, Executive Editor, desiringGod.org;
Author, *The Christmas We Didn't Expect*

"Fire your imagination with this story full of wonder, amazement, confusion and shock as you look through they eyes of Mary, Joseph and Zechariah at the first Christmas."

ED DREW, Director, Faith in Kids;
Author, *The Adventure of Christmas*

THE PROMISE AND THE LIGHT

A CHRISTMAS RETELLING

KATY MORGAN

thegoodbook
COMPANY

Katy Morgan is an Editor at The Good Book Company. She likes climbing hills and exploring new places—both in books and in real life! Before Katy joined TGBC she used to work in a school, and now she teaches the Bible every week to children at her church. She also reads ancient Greek and has a master's degree in Classics from Cambridge University.

The Promise and the Light
© The Good Book Company, 2021

Published by:
The Good Book Company

thegoodbook.com | thegoodbook.co.uk
thegoodbook.com.au | thegoodbook.co.nz | thegoodbook.co.in

Cover and design by André Parker | Internal illustrations by Alex Webb-Peploe

ISBN: 9781784986612 | Printed in the UK

Contents

Into the Darkness

The land was burning. Every door had been battered down, every field and farm had been trampled: the vines uprooted, the crops stripped from their furrows. The streets in the towns echoed with the laughter of enemy soldiers and the wails of the conquered.

Israel had been a land of promise, once. The Israelites had been led there by their God. They had settled, grown crops, raised children, fought wars, won victories... They had been a mighty nation, a contented people. But now blood seeped through the ground and fire crackled in the air. Thousands were led away as captives. All that remained was distress and fearful gloom.

And yet...

Into the darkness came—not light, no, not yet. But a promise. It came on the lips of a messenger from God, a man named Isaiah, who had said,

> *"The people walking in darkness have seen a great light; on those living in the land of deep darkness, a light has dawned."*

Those who heard it lifted up their eyes in hope—and wondered when the words would come true.

Years passed. Captivity ended. The people straggled back to their fields and farms, rebuilt their towns and cities, grew crops, raised children. They fought wars, too, but they lost them. They praised God, but he seemed far away. The streets still resounded with cruel laughter. The darkness remained.

The years became centuries.

Still they waited. Not all of them, no, but some. There had been a promise, and it gave hope to those who remembered it.

There was still so much darkness. But one day... one day, the promise said, there would be light.

CHAPTER 1

The First Moment of the Rest of My Life

Joseph

"Let's go, then," said my brother Josiah as he stowed his tools in the back of the cart. He was scowling impatiently because our father was just sitting there, not moving, not getting ready to head back to Nazareth where we lived, but reminiscing about Bethlehem instead.

"A place to be proud of," he was saying, all misty-eyed. "The city of our ancestors since all the way back before the time of captivity—back even before the time of kings…" He shook his head. "Perhaps I should never have left."

Josiah was glaring at me. Which I suppose was fair enough. It was my fault: I was the one who'd brought up the topic of Bethlehem. I was curious because I'd never been there—and because now it sounded like, before the year was out, I would finally get the chance.

I'd heard the news a few hours before. I was high up on the scaffolding of the half-built bathhouse we were working on, and there was a group of old women talking below. I wasn't paying any attention to them until they all spoke the same word at once.

"Census!"

This sounded interesting. Carefully, slowly, I put down my tools, wincing as the hammer clunked against the planks. But the women below showed no sign of having heard. I leaned out towards them.

It was obvious which of them had brought the news; even from above I could see the gleam of triumph in her eye at being the first to know. "My great-nephew's wife's cousin's friend is high up in the army and he says they're already preparing for it. The Emperor wants to know who is in his empire—a list of names and numbers from every province."

"So he can take more tax off us, I suppose," answered one of the others, and they all muttered angrily.

"But when will this census be, my dear?" asked another. I watched the gleam fade from the first woman's face: she didn't know. "I expect they'll announce it soon," she said, then brightened: "Very soon, if they're making preparations already."

"It'll be chaos," said the woman who had complained about tax. "Hardly anyone still lives in the places their families come from these days. And they'll all have to go back." She seemed rather pleased about this.

Go back to where our families came from! If that was true, it meant we'd have to travel to Bethlehem, my parents and brother and I. All the rest of our family was there—and always had been, for generations, right back to King David himself. I felt excitement rising in me.

But the old women were murmuring again. I knelt down and leaned a bit further out, trying to hear. Why had they dropped their voices? What else were they saying? If I could just get a little closer—and a little bit more—

"Aaargh!" I flailed in the air, losing my balance for a moment, my hands scrabbling to find something to hold onto. Feeling the roughness of wood, I gripped the scaffolding planks with relief and scuffled backwards, breathing heavily.

"That was close." I peered over the edge again. Every one of the old women was fixing me with an angry stare.

"Eavesdropping, boy?"

"No!" I shouted, too loudly, picking up my hammer and waving it at them. "Nearly dropped this! Not eavesdropping! Have a good day, ladies!"

They tutted and moved away. I went back to work. But I was thinking about Bethlehem all the rest of that day.

I'd never been to Bethlehem. I had never travelled anywhere much, really—except to Sepphoris, where we went every day, rattling back and forth in our donkey-cart. We were carpenters, and Sepphoris was a proper town with plenty of building work to be had, not like Nazareth where no one could afford to pay you much for anything. So my father said it was worth the journey. But that was the furthest I ever really had cause to go. Bethlehem seemed almost as far away as the stars.

"I didn't know what I was losing when I left," my father said, still sitting on the donkey-cart and not going anywhere. "Of course, I gained wonderful things... your mother, and the two of you... but I should have taken you back there. We mustn't forget where we come from."

Josiah coughed pointedly, prodding me in the back. He nodded towards Boaz, the donkey, who was standing solidly in front of us. I took the hint: pulling the stick gently out of my father's hand, I struck Boaz on the rump to get him going. Josiah grunted in satisfaction and settled himself down in the back of the cart.

"Do you know why I called that donkey Boaz?" said my father suddenly.

"Yes, Ba—" I said, but it was too late to stop him.

"Not long before our ancestor David was born, the people had no king," he began. "The Lord God raised up leaders here and there, but everyone did whatever they pleased. There was murder, violence—everything was rotten—people stealing from each other, taking advantage of each other, acting with great cruelty—"

"Nothing like today, then," cut in Josiah drily.

My father ignored him. "But in Bethlehem there lived a man of strength and justice. Boaz."

"The great-grandfather of King David," I said.

"A man," Ba went on, "who, when he saw a woman in need, did everything he could to help and protect her."

We all knew the story. He was talking about Ruth: a foreign woman, not one of God's people, who came to Bethlehem poor and almost completely friendless. Boaz helped her, and in the end he married her.

"Boaz and Ruth had a son, Obed," my father continued, while Josiah groaned in irritation behind us, "and their son had a son, and he had a son—well, he had many sons, but the most important was David, who became our people's greatest king."

"We know," said Josiah in a flat voice.

My mother's name was Ruth, too. When Ba first called the donkey Boaz, she had hit him around the head with a cooking pot and told him she'd never felt more insulted. But the name stuck even so. Boaz the donkey was definitely strong, although I'm not sure he was a fine example of virtue and justice. In fact, he was quite lazy.

I raised my stick to tap him across the hindquarters again and he clattered forward reluctantly.

Ba turned to me. "Joseph, it's time you thought about having sons yourself."

"Wha—?" I almost dropped the stick.

"I mean it," my father said. "You're old enough to get married now. I'd like some grandchildren. Some little Davids running around."

Josiah sniggered.

"After all," said Ba, "one day a descendant of King David's will sit on the throne again. Who knows which descendant that'll be?"

My brother spluttered in amazement. "What are you hoping for—that King Herod will adopt one of your *little Davids* and make him the next king?" He laughed scornfully. "Maybe if Joseph has a particularly handsome little son, the Roman Emperor himself will make him his heir."

"Well, of course not—"

"I think we should choose our own king, not sit around waiting for one to appear," declared Josiah. He gazed at the hills ahead of us. Beyond them, I knew, his mind's eye saw Jerusalem, the great city far away in the south.

"That's rebel talk," answered my father sharply. "The king is Herod. And he pays your wages."

Josiah didn't reply. Ba turned back to me. "Is there no one you've thought of?" he asked. "No one you like?"

I could feel my face burning with embarrassment. Of course there was. Of course there was only one person I could ever think of marrying. But I'd never confessed it to anyone.

I took a deep breath. Now was the moment. The first moment of the rest of my life.

"Yes," I said. "I know who I want to marry."

And when I heard what the old women were gossiping about the next day, it was the perfect excuse to go and see her.

CHAPTER 2

Things Like That Don't Happen Anymore

Mary

Joseph could have had a pack of dogs chasing him, he was running so fast. His sandals flapped against his feet as he tore through the almond grove. If my mother had been there, she would have told him to fasten them a bit better.

But I just smiled and waited for him to collapse in a heap.

"Mary!" he shouted again as he sped closer. "Mary!"

He broke off and bent over with his hands on his knees, panting.

"It's Elizabeth!"

Elizabeth? My smile slipped. If I'd been expecting to hear some news, it wasn't about my great-aunt. "What?" I cried. "Is she ill? Has there been an accident?

Is it Zechariah? Elizabeth always says those roads are dangerous..."

Zechariah was Elizabeth's husband. He was a priest, so he had to go away sometimes to serve in the great temple of the Lord. Elizabeth wanted him to do his duty, of course (she was very proud of him), but I knew she worried when he was away.

Now I was worried too. "Has something happened? Tell me!"

But Joseph shook his head at my rush of questions. "It's good news," he said. "I just wanted to be the first one to tell you. Your aunt Elizabeth is..."

He paused dramatically.

I folded my arms.

"Pregnant!" He flung out his hands with an air of triumph.

What?

"That's ridiculous," I said. "Elizabeth is..." I didn't know how to put it without being rude. "Well, she's..."

"Far too old." Joseph was nodding earnestly. "But you know I'm working in Sepphoris at the moment? I keep hearing these old women gossiping. I heard them yesterday as well..."—he hesitated—"I'll tell you about that another time. But today they were talking about Elizabeth."

He was serious about this; I could see it in his eyes. He really believed that my elderly great-aunt was going to have a baby.

"What did they say?" I asked cautiously.

"They said—well, they weren't very polite. You know what people have said about her in the past."

"That she's cursed."

"Yes, and that she's a disgrace to her family."

I could feel myself getting cross. "Just because she's never had a baby!"

Poor Elizabeth. She'd watched everyone around her—all the friends she'd grown up with—have children, when she couldn't. Then she'd watched those children grow up and have their own children. She was always cradling other people's babies, always chasing after other people's toddlers, always hearing the chanting of children at their lessons. Yet she'd never had a baby of her own. And people whispered behind their hands that God must be punishing her for something. Hadn't she been through enough without that kind of talk?

Joseph was looking at me apprehensively, waiting to see whether I'd start getting all indignant. I contained myself and fell silent instead.

"But if she's pregnant now…" he said gently.

I grinned. "They'll have to take it all back."

"These old women I overheard didn't know what to think," Joseph told me. "One of them was saying she must be making it up. Then another one insisted her niece had seen her with her own eyes. Round belly and everything."

"Do you really think it's true?"

"If I didn't, I wouldn't have run all the way here to tell you!" He plonked himself down on the ground with a sigh and started rubbing his feet. "Your great-aunt wouldn't fake it, would she?"

"Of course not."

"Then it must be true." He looked up at me again. "By the way... I have something to ask you."

He looked serious. I sat down next to him, waiting.

"You, er... Well, I..." He coughed. "Um, you wouldn't happen to have any of those nice honey cakes your mother makes?"

I laughed. His news might be strange, but some things would never change: Joseph would always be hungry.

I decided to save the news until later, when the whole family was gathered around the fire for dinner. Everyone was quiet: my brothers were busy stuffing themselves with soup-soaked bread, and Ma was ladling portions into bowls for my little sister Abigail and me while my father poured out the water.

"Joseph came today," I said brightly, "and told me that Elizabeth and Zechariah are going to have a baby."

My mother stared at me, soup dripping off her spoon. "What?"

"He heard some women in Sepphoris talking about it. One of them has a niece who's seen her."

"Mary," said my father patiently, "that cannot be true. Women cannot fall pregnant at Elizabeth's age."

I was ready for this. "Well, Sarah did." They couldn't argue with the old stories of our people. "She and Abraham were even older than Elizabeth and Zechariah when she became pregnant. And Hannah was the same: Samuel the prophet was born to her even though no one thought she could ever have a child."

"Sarah and Hannah lived a long time ago," Ma told me. "Things like that don't happen anymore."

"Why not? Why couldn't they?"

"Well…" Her lips pressed together impatiently as she passed Abigail her bowl. "Those babies were a special gift from God. And they were born centuries ago, Mary! Sarah and Abraham lived before our nation was even a nation. Things are different now."

"I don't see why. God could give special gifts again."

"He doesn't do things like that these days," chipped in Reuben, my older brother. He ran a hand through his hair. "He doesn't care about us."

"Reuben!" said Ba, angry. "He cares very much about us."

"How do you know?"

"Because he has promised."

It was the kind of thing Zechariah would have said. Ba took another mouthful and I waited while he chewed, wondering if he'd say more. His eyes were closed; maybe he was thinking about all the wonderful promises God had made, or all the stories of the things he'd done? Perhaps he was about to explain to us how we were part of God's chosen nation; how, even though we had been ruled by a string of other peoples across hundreds of years, we were still God's prized possession, the children of Abraham. And one day things would come good again.

That's what Zechariah would have done. When I was little and he visited more often, he would take me on his knee and tell me stories of all that God had done and all that he had promised to do. Zechariah knew everything there was to know about the Scriptures and he loved God with all his heart, all his soul, and all his strength. Even though he had no children of his own, even though he had to leave Elizabeth alone sometimes in order to do his job, and even though Jerusalem was filled with soldiers nowadays and everyone said that once King Herod died the Romans would take over entirely, Zechariah always believed that God had a plan.

"He has promised…" he used to tell me, tapping his nose and smiling affectionately while I wriggled on his lap or pulled at his long beard. Then he would begin a story.

But when Ba said, "He has promised…" he didn't have anything to add. He finished chewing and opened his eyes to see us all looking at him expectantly.

He cleared his throat. "What are you all looking at? Go on, eat your dinner."

Then my mother sighed loudly. "Oh, Abigail." My sister had food all down her front.

"I dropped a piece of bread after I dipped it in the soup," she giggled.

"More than one piece, by the look of it," I said, and went to get a cloth.

After that everyone forgot the subject of Elizabeth and Zechariah. Until the day the letter came.

CHAPTER 3

A Particular Kind of Laugh

Mary

I'd been with my sister Abigail all day, sitting under the big old oak tree in the middle of Nazareth.

It was fun sitting there, even if we were doing chores. Wool-spinning was less boring in the middle of the village. We used to watch the boys who were studying at the synagogue, playing soldiers during their breaks between lessons with branches for swords. Or the flocks of goats that herdsmen would bring through. I could never tell how they knew whose animals were whose, because every single one was brown with white spots. The goats strutted and bleated their way through the village and we had to stuff our work under our skirts to keep it from the clouds of dust billowing beneath their hooves.

That day, Jakin had managed to get loose—Joanna's donkey. He burst down the street with a triumphant HEE HAW and bucked exactly like the boys from the synagogue, celebrating when they landed a good sword-strike. Eventually he came over to rest in the shade and Abigail stroked his face, while I grabbed hold of the rope around his neck. He drooped his muzzle to the ground as I led him back down the street to Joanna.

"Oh, Mary, thank you!" she shouted over the sound of her husband's trundling pottery wheel. "Here, I've just been baking. Are you hungry?"

The loaf she gave me was quite small. But it was still nice of her. I took it back to Abigail and we munched away.

But Nathan, my little brother, had just come out of the synagogue, and he barrelled up to us. "Can I have some?" He tried to snatch the loaf from Abigail's hands.

"Stop—" I cried, but it was too late. She'd pushed him away and now they were both sprawling on the ground—along with most of Abigail's wool.

"Nathan!" I said angrily, starting to pick it up. Then I dropped it all again. Abigail had started choking. She must have been halfway through a mouthful and it had got stuck in her throat. Her face was going pinker and pinker, her hands fluttering helplessly in the air.

I slapped her on the back. She gave one huge cough, then began to take big shuddering gulps, chest heaving.

Her eyes were big and wide and panicked. Tears flooded down her face. But she was breathing.

Nathan had picked himself up and mooched away, back to his lessons. I put my arm round Abigail's shoulders, relieved that she was all right. "Cheer up! Look, I'll tell you why our ancestors Abraham and Sarah named their son Isaac, which means Laugh. But—" I poked her— "only if you smile!"

It worked. A grin started to compete with the tears on her face. So we settled ourselves back down, and I began.

Later I thought it was funny that I told this particular story on that particular day. I'd been thinking about Sarah and Abraham already, of course, because of the gossip Joseph had heard. But telling the story properly to my sister made me think about it more—and it helped me to make sense of things afterwards.

"There are different kinds of laughter," I told Abigail. "Happy laughter. Silly laughter. Mean laughter. And laughter you just can't help, like when someone tickles you. But none of these was the kind of laugh which our ancestor Sarah laughed when she heard she was going to have a son."

Abi nestled into me as she always did when I was telling a story. The tears had gone now. I spoke low so that only she could hear. "Our ancestors didn't live like we live now, in houses made of brick and stone," I said. "Abraham and Sarah lived in a big tent which they took with them from place to place. One day they had pitched it in Mamre, far away on the other side of Jerusalem. There were huge old oak trees there and you could sit beneath their shade."

My sister looked up at our own tree. I could see what was in her imagination: Abraham and Sarah, sitting with us beneath the twisting branches, patting a donkey while their tent flaps flapped in the breeze.

"Sarah and Abraham were very old," I went on. "They had wanted a child of their own for a very long time. And God had promised them a son. But the promise had never come true. And now Sarah believed it never would.

"Then one day three visitors came."

"The Lord! The Lord!" interrupted Abigail. I must have told her the story before sometime, I realised.

"Yes," I said, "we're told that it was the Lord God himself who was their visitor. Abraham didn't know this at first. Even so, he welcomed these strange figures kindly."

"He gave them food," Abi offered.

"Milk and meat and cheese curds," I agreed, "and Sarah kneaded dough and baked bread to soak up the milk and the meat juices. But she stayed inside the tent, while Abraham took the food out to the guests."

"Why?"

"I don't know," I admitted. "Maybe she was tired from all the kneading. Maybe she was shy. Maybe she thought they wouldn't want her there. But she sat behind the tent-flap and listened to everything the men said."

To do the Lord's voice, I tried to sound deep and booming. "The Lord God said, 'Your wife Sarah will soon have a son.' And behind the tent flap, Sarah said to herself, A son? When I'm old? She couldn't help but scoff at that. She burst out laughing. It was not happy laughter. It was not mean laughter. It was…" I couldn't find the right word.

"Angry," said Abigail.

"Ye-ess," I replied slowly. "Or… bitter. Sour. She knew it was impossible that she could have a child now. Why would God promise such a thing?

"Anyway, the Lord God heard her laughing, of course. And he said again"—I put on the booming voice—"'Your wife Sarah will soon have a son.' Then the three figures got up and went away.

"After that, Abraham and Sarah took down their tent and left the shady oaks of Mamre. They went through the desert where the sand howled in their faces. They had adventures and escaped danger. And one year after they had met with the Lord God, Sarah gave birth to a son."

Abigail wriggled happily. "Isaac!"

"When the child was born," I nodded, "they named him Isaac, which means Laugh, because they were so happy to have a son. Every time they looked at his chubby little face, they smiled and laughed. God had kept his promise! And Sarah said, 'God has made me laugh, and everyone who hears about it will laugh too.'"

"Ho, ho, ho," went Abigail obligingly. The sight of her, holding her sides like a jolly old man, pretending to laugh, made me burst out in genuine laughter—and soon we were both wiping away tears.

"And," I said, concluding my story, "Isaac grew up and had sons of his own, and they had sons, and eventually there was a whole nation, a great people that still exists today, even though it's a bit scattered and divided. And you and I are part of that people. The children of Abraham."

As I spoke, the boys ran out of the synagogue again for the end of the day.

"Time to go home," I said, swinging my wool basket onto my back and catching Nathan to make him carry Abi's. It was a punishment for earlier, but both of them seemed to have forgotten what had happened. They were soon racing ahead of me and I decided not to chase them. I was imagining my great-aunt Elizabeth laughing. I could just picture the worry-lines on her face fading away.

By the time I reached the almond field, Nathan and Abigail had disappeared into the house, and all was peaceful. The tree branches rustled and I paused, looking up into their shade, wondering whether God really was going to give my great-aunt and uncle a child.

But the peace was soon shattered—by my mother, of all people.

She ran towards me—actually ran—and I saw a letter rolled up in her hand.

"Mary," she panted, "Mary, it's true."

"What?" I cried, able to think of one thing only: "Elizabeth?"

"Elizabeth," she nodded. "Yes. My aunt Elizabeth is actually pregnant at last."

CHAPTER 4

The Figure in the Temple

Zechariah

In my letters to my family I was brief. I simply explained that by an extraordinary and unexpected gift of God, my wife Elizabeth had fallen pregnant and would give birth in the summer.

Of how I discovered it—how I knew that it would take place, many weeks before the first physical signs of it became obvious to Elizabeth herself—I told them nothing. It was a secret too strange and holy, too precious and wondrous, to share. I only told young Mary of it, months later, and then she told Joseph.

But I will tell of it now.

Most of my duties as a priest of the Lord take place in the outer courts of the temple: speaking with the people, taking their offerings of grain or money, performing sacrifices, directing the temple servants. But on that particular occasion, my name was drawn to enter into the temple itself.

No priest takes this duty lightly. I was trembling as I passed through the doors—and not, I hasten to add, because of my age. Before me was the great curtain which divides the first section of the temple from the second. Behind the curtain God's presence is so powerful that it could burn me to a crisp to enter. But even the first section is a holy and precious place.

I had the incense ready. I should have gone straight to the altar in front of the curtain, set the scented powder alight, paused to see that the smoke was rising as it should, and made my exit.

But I could not.

Instead I froze. And then fell to my knees.

There was a figure beside the altar.

He was huge—taller than any man. A blinding brightness seemed to pour out of him, so that his outline was hard to see, as though he wasn't a separate being at all but part of the temple somehow, of one substance with its golden surfaces and polished stone. Yet at the same time he seemed utterly solid, as though he had been there long before anything else.

And he was not a man. I had thrown my hands over my eyes but through my fingers I saw that he had six wings like the wings of eagles: long and broad and dense with shining feathers. Each wingtip stretched to the edge of the room, the feathers brushing against the walls.

He looked at me. The silence was as hard as marble.

My incense was scattered all over the floor, but I did not dare move to gather it up.

Then the angel said, "Do not be afraid, Zechariah. Your prayer has been heard. Your wife Elizabeth will bear you a son, and you are to call him John."

I sucked in my breath.

Elizabeth and I had been praying for a child for a long, long time. But I was already old, and Elizabeth… well, she was getting on in years. We still prayed, but we no longer really believed it would ever happen.

The angel was speaking again: "Many will rejoice because of his birth… He will bring back many to the Lord their God… He will go on before the Lord in the spirit and power of Elijah…"

But I was barely listening. "How can I be sure?" I heard myself blurt out. Fool! The thought of it still covers me with shame. To doubt the word of such a figure, a creature like no man, a messenger from the Lord himself! What was I thinking? Who was I to suggest he was mistaken?

The angel's response was like the roar of a lion—no, like a thousand lions, all roaring at once. "I am Gabriel!" he bellowed. "I stand in the presence of God. I have been sent to tell you this good news!"

Then his voice became quieter—which was somehow even more terrifying. "Now," he said, while I trembled before him, my hands grasping helplessly at the unfriendly floor, "you will be silent and unable to speak until the day the child is born, because you did not believe my words."

And he was gone, and the room was filled with smoke.

If I had not believed at first, I certainly did after that. When I staggered out of the temple, my mouth was opening and closing like a gulping fish. I could say nothing. I could make no sound. I had become utterly speechless.

The other priests and the temple servants were waiting for me outside. I could see the concern on their faces: why had I taken so long? Placing the incense on the altar was a holy and honourable task, but a simple one.

When they saw my dishevelled clothes and shocked face, my silent mouth and my eyes still blinking from the brightness of the angel, it was not hard for them to guess that something extraordinary had happened. They were desperate to know what I had seen and what it might mean for the future of our people.

But I could tell them nothing.

For a while I believe I was in shock. I was no great man, no mighty king or inspired prophet... I was not wealthy or distinguished... yet I had seen one who was able to stand in the very presence of God. The Lord had heard our prayers—he had taken notice of us—he had sent his messenger to us. The thought of it alone brought me to my knees all over again.

When Elizabeth came to me with bright eyes some weeks later and told me that she was indeed pregnant, I was filled with a joy which I did not believe could be increased. I was wrong, of course: when John was born, it would be far greater.

The angel had predicted that, too. While I cowered on the floor in the temple wondering how his words could possibly come true, I heard his mighty voice saying, "He will be a delight to you." And then he added, "And many will rejoice because of his birth, for he will be great in the sight of the Lord."

This was the first source of my pleasure. The angel said that this child—my son—would be great in the Lord's eyes. God's own Spirit would fill him—and was already filling him, even before he was born. He would be a prophet, speaking God's own words. He would lead our people back to the ways of God.

These were the promises that the angel made. I swear that I tell no lie.

CHAPTER 5

There'll Be a Reason

Mary

"What d'you think it means?" I asked.

Nathan had been sent to wash and Abigail and I were sorting through the work we'd done that day, gathering up the piles of coarse wool and the spun yarn and putting it all away in big baskets. Ma was supervising Abi, slapping her hand when she was careless, sighing as she noticed a hole in one of the baskets.

"Something special," said Abigail, sitting back with an unusually serious expression on her face. "God made it happen."

Ma pursed her lips. "Maybe so," she said carefully.

Just then Reuben came in, closely followed by Josiah, Joseph's younger brother. Reuben stomped across the room and seized the loaf of bread from the table, tearing off a big strip and stuffing it into his mouth. He handed another to Josiah.

"Reuben!" exclaimed my mother. "Not with dirty hands!"

Josiah put his piece of bread down and wiped his hands quickly. But Reuben pulled a face and went on chewing.

Ma raised her eyebrows.

Slowly, slowly, with a sneer, Reuben wiped his hands on his clothes. Each finger left its own broad track of dirt.

My mother shook her head. "Have you heard the news?"

"Yeah," he grunted. "So what? It's just a baby. Another mouth to feed." He swallowed, took a drink of water straight out of the jug, then wiped his mouth with the back of his hand.

"But there'll be a *reason*—" said Abigail before I could shush her.

"Of course there isn't!" cried my brother, suddenly animated. He ran his hands through his hair. "What, you think *God* has specifically chosen our aunt and uncle to have some kind of special child? Of course he hasn't."

"But..." Abigail's bottom lip was quivering. "But it's like Sarah and Abraham."

"Look," said Reuben, "maybe God really did do all those things years and years ago. Maybe he really did speak to Abraham and Moses and Elijah and give children to people and win battles and make cities crumble and choose kings and all the rest of it. I'm not saying he didn't. But he doesn't do that now. We're on our own. For goodness' sake, Abigail, don't be such a baby. There is no deep meaning in things. Zechariah and Elizabeth just got lucky."

Abigail was now in real danger of bursting into tears. "Stop it," I said to my brother.

"You're the one that needs to stop it, Mary," he spat. "Filling her head with all those stories. She needs to live in the real world. The world of harsh winters and rocky fields and—and bread that doesn't taste of anything." He glanced down at the loaf beside him with a grimace.

"Some people don't have any bread at all, young man," began my mother indignantly, and Reuben groaned.

"That's exactly my point," he said. "We're supposed to be God's chosen people, but we're poor. We're like—like dirt on someone's shoe. And meanwhile the Romans run everything and the Greeks live in the lap of luxury, practically on our doorstep." He threw up his hands. "What's the point of going on about the past when now is such a complete nightmare?"

Josiah, who'd stayed silent so far, was nodding eagerly. "It's time to act," he said. "Reuben, this is what I've been telling you. We need a new king. All we have to do is go—"

But Reuben kicked his friend before he could finish his sentence. He shoved Josiah out of the door, shaking his head, and then went out himself. He paused before ducking under the lintel. "Don't take that idiot seriously," he said. "New king indeed." He spat on the ground. "Seems to me it would be better just not to be part of our people at all."

My rock was large and flattish and much more comfortable than it looked. I always sat here when I wanted to be alone, walking just a little way uphill from the house and settling myself down where no one could see me. I was listening to the insects in the trees and enjoying the cool evening air on my face, trying to forget the cross words and tears and tensions back in the house.

"There is no rock like our God," I found myself singing softly as I leaned back against the stone. What was the rest of the tune? I hummed it, and gradually the words threaded themselves together in my mind, remembered from some synagogue service or childhood lesson. "There is no one holy like the Lord, there is no one besides you, there is no rock like our God."

What song was it, I wondered? Who sang that song first? I kept singing—then broke off as my heart thudded. "Of course," I whispered. "It's Hannah's song."

It was a strange coincidence. Hannah was another woman in the old stories who thought she would never have children. She was taunted, disgraced, unhappy, just like my great-aunt. Desperate. And when she went to pray for a child, the priest assumed she was drunk and told her off.

But God heard her prayer and loved her, and she had a son, and named him Samuel.

I sang her song all the way through. Then I sang the last lines again. "He will give strength to his king." An odd thing for Hannah to say, I suddenly thought, because God's people didn't even have a king at that point.

Pondering, I looked up to see my Ba standing over me. He had a strange smile on his face, sort of sad and affectionate at the same time.

"Samuel was given to Hannah," I told him, "and he was special. When he grew up he was the one who crowned the first kings of Israel. Hannah sang about it—she knew about it, or imagined it somehow, even when Samuel was only a tiny baby. She knew that that was what God gave him to her for. He came to prepare the way for a king."

I looked into his face, wondering if he'd know what I was getting at—that maybe Zechariah's child would be the same, that he would come to prepare the way for something. That he was special, like Samuel.

But Ba just said, "Yes, that's a good story." He took my hand and pulled me to my feet. "Mary, I have some news that concerns you."

"Me?" My heart thudded again. Why was Ba's face so serious?

"I've been speaking to Joseph's father," he began.

And that was how I found out that Joseph and I would be married.

CHAPTER 6

Josiah's Missing

Joseph

On the day of the betrothal I was awake and upright before anyone else had opened their eyes. I sawed a hunk of bread from the previous day's loaf and paced around chewing it. I put on my best tunic, which my mother had washed specially, then changed my mind and switched it for the ordinary work one. I paced around some more. I stood up and sat down a few times. Then I decided to go and fetch water from the well. Normally that was my mother's job, but she was still asleep and I needed to be busy.

There were a few women there already and they laughed as I drew near.

"Will you fetch water for your wife when you're married, Joseph?" called one of them.

"I wish I had a husband like you," said another.

I fumbled to fix the jar to the rope, embarrassed.

Eventually my fingers and thumbs managed to tie the knot. I let the jar down into the well until I heard a splash. Then I hauled it back up again.

It was heavy. I tried to lift it up onto my head like the women do, but it slopped everywhere, tipping water all down the back of my neck. Good thing I'd changed my tunic.

Now there were more women arriving, and every single one of them was laughing at me. I stood there foolishly, shivering, then picked up the jar again, hugging it against my chest this time and hoping it wouldn't slip out of my grasp.

"Joseph." My mother had appeared, tutting. She took the jar off me and swung it smoothly onto her head, steadying it there with one sun-browned hand. Then she set off home. I stumbled after her, feeling like an idiot.

"You're up early," my mother said. "Where did your brother go?"

"Josiah? I don't know," I answered. "He was asleep when I left. Is he not now?"

"No." She pressed her lips together but said nothing else.

When we were home and I had spent a bit more time pacing up and down, my mother tutted again and sent me out. "Go and see if Mary's mother needs anything for the meal," she told me. "And if you see your brother, tell him he must not be late."

I went around the edge of the village so as to avoid passing the well again, and was soon walking up through the almond grove to where Mary's house sat on the rising hill. Her mother was outside, kneading dough; Abigail sat beside her. The little girl started giggling excitedly when she saw me.

"Joseph!" said Mary's mother, looking surprised. "You're not all coming already?"

"No, no," I said, trying to be respectful and not to look at Abigail, who was beginning to dance around, clapping her hands and moving slowly like she was wearing heavy wedding clothes.

"You'll dance like this," she whispered, "and we'll all sing and clap our hands like that…"

"Stop that, Abi," said her mother. "They're not getting married yet. It's just the betrothal."

This was what had been agreed: we would pledge ourselves to one another today, and I would give money and gifts to Mary and her family. Then we would all celebrate with a meal. In a year's time, once I had built an extra room on my parents' house, we would be married and Mary would officially become part of my family.

"I just came to ask if there was anything you need," I said to Mary's mother as Abigail sat down again. "For the meal, I mean. Ma sent me."

"Ah," she said, "no, I think we have everything."

She went on kneading. I hovered uncertainly.

"Mary's gone to fetch water," said Abigail with a knowing grin.

"And when she comes back she has a lot to do," added her mother. "As do we all. Abigail, could you fetch Reuben, please? I have a job for him."

But Abigail came back almost at once, shrugging. "Not there," she said.

"Josiah's missing too," I said, biting my lip.

"Oh, may the Lord help us," cried Mary's mother. She cast her eyes to the sky. "Those two!"

But she had nothing more to say, and I went off, feeling unwelcome.

At last it was time. We set off, just the three of us, my father grumbling a little about how we live too far away from my uncle and the rest of the family. "If only they could have come," he said, while my mother muttered something about how if Josiah didn't turn up, he'd be in big trouble. We walked through the village, drawing admiring glances from everyone we passed.

"May the Lord bless you," said an old man, bowing at me.

"May he build up your family," nodded Joanna the potter's wife, a little further along. My mother beamed at her.

Soon we were there. The whole crowd of Mary's family were standing outside her house: her father's sisters and their husbands and children, her mother's brother and his family, her grandmother leaning on a twisted stick… her mother and father, coming forward to meet us… her sister and two brothers… and Mary herself, standing in the midst of them dressed in deep blue with a thin shawl the colour of ripened wheat around her head and shoulders.

She caught my eye. I felt some of the tension leave my body.

But my mother was looking elsewhere. "Reuben is there," she hissed. "Where's Josiah?"

Nowhere to be seen. Meanwhile Reuben skulked behind his uncle, looking shifty.

My mother marched straight up to him, ignoring the greetings of Mary's parents. Mary's ma raised her eyebrows and my heart sank. It was going wrong already.

"Where's my boy?" Ma demanded, jabbing her finger at Reuben' chest.

He shrank back, unusually shy, avoiding her gaze.

"I know you know where he is. Come on, out with it."

Then Reuben stammered, "He's gone. He went—he's gone to Judea."

"*Judea?*"

"I thought about going with him," muttered Reuben, "but I—I came back." He ran his hand through his hair, uncharacteristically nervous.

I didn't wait to hear any more. I just ran.

I didn't even pause. Was it because I was desperate for my brother to be at the betrothal? Or was it because I

knew that if he really did go off all the way to the south-
ern part of the kingdom, he'd probably never make it
back? To be honest, I don't even know. I didn't stop for
long enough to think anything through.

"Changed your mind?" someone called out as I left
the village. But I barely heard. There was only one road
out of Nazareth that led southwards, and I followed it,
feet pounding in the dust, running harder than I'd ever
run before.

My best clothes were ruined and my whole body
drenched with sweat before my thoughts arranged
themselves properly and I slowed to a walk, realising I
wasn't going to catch him. He must have left early in the
morning. He was hours ahead of me; even walking, he'd
be far, far away by now.

My brother was gone. Gone south, where he'd never
been before. Gone to find trouble, almost certainly.

I stopped in the middle of the road, feeling completely
foolish. The words that had followed me out of the village taunted me suddenly; they'd all think I had changed
my mind.

I might have ruined my chances with Mary for ever.

I breathed in and out a few times and then sprinted
back the way I'd come.

They were all still there. They were crowded around
the house, all of them talking at the top of their voices.
None of them saw me. I strode forwards and grasped
Mary by the hand.

She pulled a face. "Sweaty!"

Then we laughed, and everyone else started laughing too.

It was going to be all right.

CHAPTER 7

Like the End of the World

Zechariah

The Lord God has always had dealings with humans, of course, ever since the world began; but Abraham was the first to whom he swore an oath. He gave him his son Isaac, and afterwards he swore to bless him and to multiply his descendants until there were as many of them as stars in the sky or grains of sand on the seashore. He promised moreover that through these descendants every nation on earth would be blessed.

So Abraham lived and died, as did his son Isaac after him, as did his son Jacob, whose other name was Israel. By that name all our people are named, although we are also called the children of Abraham, or the Jews, or simply the people of God.

I'd always liked to rehearse the names, squeezing all that history into those few familiar words: Abraham, Isaac, Jacob, Joseph, Moses, Samuel, David, Solomon…

Since my meeting with the angel I could not speak, and I had to write them instead of saying them—but it was still a comfort. All those generations, and the Lord God had remained the same.

But my thoughts in those days kept dragging themselves back to one name in particular.

Elijah.

"In the spirit and power of Elijah," the angel had said in the temple as he spoke about my unborn son. "He will go on before the Lord, in the spirit and power of Elijah."

So my pen scratched the name again and again, pressing down so hard you'd have been able to read what I'd written even if I hadn't used ink. *ELIJAH ELIJAH ELIJAH*, carved into the parchment like an etching on stone.

What you must understand is that after King David, things went downhill for our people. God had promised that one of David's descendants would sit on the throne for ever and ever—that his kingdom would never end. But the kings who came after David did not live up to his example. They did not love God as he had. They did not lead the people as God's king should.

The worst king of all was Ahab—and it was to him that Elijah came.

ELIJAH ELIJAH ELIJAH, I wrote, my hand starting to shake with the effort. The spirit and power of Elijah.

What did that mean?

Elijah's was a story I had told many times to the boys in the synagogue. "During the reign of Ahab," I used to say, "there was a terrible famine: a time when no garden was green and even the best vineyard could not thrive. The dust gathered in the crevices of the eyes and the belly ached and the throat croaked for water. No rains came and no crops grew and there was not enough to eat. And all this was because of the wickedness of King Ahab and his wife.

"Queen Jezebel was not a child of Abraham," I'd explain, "and she did not love the Lord. She turned her husband away from the God who had given him his kingdom. The two of them worshipped the false god Baal instead, and they taught all the people to do the same. So law became lawlessness, order became chaos, and where there should have been peace there was violence."

And then I'd tell the story of Elijah.

He came to warn the king. He came with a message from God himself. But Ahab did not listen. And this was why the famine was so severe.

"At last," I'd tell the boys quietly, meeting their eyes one by one to check they were listening—and they always were—"there was a gathering of all the people. Elijah stood before them and told them to make up their minds. 'If the Lord is God,' he cried out, 'follow him. But if Baal is God, follow him.'

"But they did not answer. They would not say who they would follow."

I'd pause for a few heartbeats here, dropping my gaze, hoping that the boys would be asking themselves the question: what would I have said? And that their answer would be "The Lord".

Then I'd go on. "So Elijah held a contest there on the mountaintop. They all agreed the way it would work. It was simple: there would be two piles of wood, and the god who was truly God would be the one to send fire and set the wood ablaze.

"The priests of Baal danced and shouted," I'd say, raising my arms and twirling my fingers a little. "They begged and prayed. They cut themselves with swords and spears to get their god's attention. But Baal made no answer. No fire came.

"Then Elijah had men bring great jars and drench his own pile of wood with water so that no one could set it alight. They poured the water once, twice, three times. The people watched. They had still not decided which god they would follow.

"Elijah said, 'Lord, let it be known that you are God in Israel'. He prayed, 'Answer me, so that these people will know that you, Lord, are God, and that you are turning their hearts back again'.

"Then, like a sigh or a whisper or a sudden breeze, the fire fell."

Have you ever seen a tree falling, a tree that had seemed to be strong? At first there is a soft creak, nothing to disturb you. Then comes the almighty groan and crash that sends birds spinning into the air and causes the little creatures of the earth to quake in their burrows.

That's how I imagine it was when the fire fell on the mountain. As if the world was ending.

"So," I'd say in a whisper, "the people said, 'The Lord—he is God!' and determined to worship only him. And after that the first cloud appeared on the horizon and the rain began to fall."

Then I'd clap my hands suddenly and all the boys would jump in shock—they were always so absorbed in the story—and I'd laugh and send them outside to play.

The spirit and power of Elijah, I wrote again now. My son—the child who was growing day by day in my dear Elizabeth's womb—would be like *this* man.

It was God who sent the fire. But Elijah was the man he used—he was the way God turned the hearts of his people back to himself.

In our day there were some who were looking for a new king. They longed to see a David on the throne of Israel again. They desired independence and freedom. Joseph's brother Josiah, as I was to learn, was one of those.

But the truth was that God had not just promised to send a king. He had not just promised to send wise leaders or great warriors or even mighty angels like the one who came to me in the temple. He had promised to come *himself*. The Lord God Almighty, walking among us.

It would be unimaginable.

It would be like the end of the world.

And he had said—hundreds of years ago he had said—that before that day came, he would send someone ahead of him, someone to prepare the way. And that someone would be like Elijah.

And the angel said to me about my son, "He will go on before the Lord, in the spirit and power of Elijah, to make ready a people prepared for the Lord."

So this is what I was asking myself as I carved those words into the parchment, harder and harder: if my son was to be like Elijah, then what—who—was coming next?

And would he bring joy, or terror?

CHAPTER 8

Not Something a Bandit Would Say

Mary

I was tired out. It was the middle of the wheat harvest and my whole body ached from days spent bending over, picking up the stalks the reapers had cut and gathering armful after armful into big sheaves.

But instead of dragging myself home I found Joseph and asked how his ma was.

"Not well," he answered, biting his lip. "Will you come and see her?"

Since Josiah went south, his mother had barely come out of the house; she only emerged to fetch water in the mornings, and even that had had to be done by Joseph a few times. (Poor Joseph. I laughed and laughed when he told me about the visit to the well on the morning of our betrothal. But I think by this point he'd finally got over the embarrassment.)

As we walked into the village, Joseph explained that the previous evening had brought news of his brother for the first time.

"Ma sobbed all night," he said. "Someone said they saw him near the river Jordan with a couple of bandits." He shook his head. "I've never seen her like this, Mary. Even this afternoon she was still in tears. I don't know what to do."

I touched his arm in reassurance, trying to disguise the fact that I didn't really know what to do either. At least we could do our not-knowing-what-to-do together, I thought.

We found her sitting in the middle of the unswept floor, sewing up a torn tunic—one of Josiah's—and doing it very badly.

I knelt down and took up another shirt that needed mending. "At least we know where he is," I told her as I began to sew.

"But bandits, Mary! They'll kill him." She gave a little moan. "Or they'll teach him to kill."

"At least they'll know the road," said Joseph. "At least they'll help him find the way."

"But *bandits*!"

It went on like that for a while, but eventually we persuaded her to give up her sewing and go to bed. I swept the floor and tidied away the half-mended clothes. Then suddenly the tiredness struck me and I gave a huge yawn.

"I'll walk you home," said Joseph. "It'll be dark soon."

But I could see he was exhausted too. "Not dark yet though," I answered and flashed a grin before slipping out of the door. "See you tomorrow!"

I'd been trying to be cheery, but as I made my way back through the fields, I wished I had let him come with me. All the talk of bandits had put me on edge. It wasn't unknown for thieves to come through the village at night, after all.

It was a warm evening, but I shivered and pulled my shawl around me. I could hear a creaking and groaning among the almond trees as I came towards them. I knew it was just the wind working at the old wood, but it still made my heart beat faster.

I started singing to drown out the sound. "There is no rock like our God! My heart rejoices in the…"

My words trailed off into a whisper.

I stopped.

There was a figure standing at the edge of the almond grove. A large, male figure. It was too dark to see his face, but I was sure it wasn't my father. Or my brother.

And he seemed to be waiting for me.

I was alone. Should I run? He'd catch me up, though. Our house was a little way outside the main village and he'd catch me before I reached the safety of my neighbours' homes.

He'd seen me anyway by now. He was coming towards me. I couldn't move. *If I scream*, I thought, *my father might hear—*

But the figure reached out his hands and said, "Greetings, you who are highly favoured!"

I let out my breath.

That didn't seem like something a bandit would say.

"The Lord is with you," the figure added, and smiled.

That smile!

People sometimes say that a smile can light up the face, but I've never seen one lit up like his was. There was an actual glow: his whole face shone like a candle flame, and then it spread to the rest of his body. Around him I thought I saw the faint outline of wings, picked out by the strange light—but it was gone again when I blinked.

I stepped backwards, trembling. No, not a bandit— but what? Something even more terrifying. His face was the kindest face I ever saw, but the fiercest too, and all lit by this light that came from nowhere. I felt like I'd walked into another world.

But the dry ground crunched beneath my feet, and my fingers felt the rough fabric of my shawl, and I knew I hadn't gone anywhere. I was here, in Nazareth, and there was an *angel* in front of me, and he had called me highly favoured.

But what did that mean?

I must have looked terrified. "Do not be afraid," he told me gently.

He smiled again. The glow in his skin came back stronger than ever and his wings were clearly visible now, but I barely noticed that because what he said next was, "You will conceive and give birth to a son, and you are to call him Jesus."

The words went into my ears, but it took a moment for my mind to really hear them.

"Jesus," I mouthed weakly.

"He will be great," the angel continued, "and will be called the Son of the Most High. The Lord God will give him the throne of his father David, and he will reign over Jacob's descendants for ever." He paused as if unsure whether I'd heard him properly. "His kingdom," he added with another smile, "will never end."

So many questions clamoured for my attention. A king? The Son of the Most High God? His father David? Ruling for ever?

But the question that came out of my mouth was the simplest.

"How?" I said blankly. "I… I'm a virgin."

In other words: I had only just got betrothed. I wouldn't be married for another year. How would I have a baby?

But he spread his hands out calmly as if to show that it had all been thought of. "The power of the Most High will overshadow you," he explained, "so the holy one to be born will be called the Son of God."

My eyes widened. Believe me, if someone else had told me this I would have thought them insane. I was going to be pregnant with a baby who had no father? I was going to give birth to a child who came directly from God? Not possible.

"Even Elizabeth your relative is going to have a child in her old age," said the angel, as if that proved it. He looked at me earnestly, the light fading from his body now and concentrating in his fiery eyes. "No word from God will ever fail."

He held my gaze, and I knew—I knew it was true.

I had been right: Elizabeth's child would be special. But the most important child of all would be... would be mine.

I would have a son, and he would be God's king, and he would be God's own son.

I'll be honest, it was quite a lot to take in.

So I just nodded.

"I am the Lord's servant," I whispered. "May your word to me be fulfilled."

CHAPTER 9

A Mistake

Joseph

I was still worried about my ma. Mary came as often as she could but she couldn't do everything.

I was worried about work, too. My father and I had to slog and slog now that we didn't have Josiah. The days seemed to get longer and more exhausting, and yet have less and less time in them to do things.

And I was worried about my stupid brother out there somewhere in the south with bandits and criminals.

So I was sleeping badly. And that made everything even worse.

In Sepphoris I yawned my way through each day, just about managing not to drop any hammers on passers-by or injure myself with a mistimed scrape of the saw. But it wouldn't last. It wasn't really a surprise when I heard the foreman call my father and me over with an angry voice.

"These ceiling beams," he snapped, nodding up at the long planks which were to support the upper floor of the building. "Explain."

We peered up and I groaned. There were long cracks in three or four of the beams. We'd miscalculated somewhere: these would bear no weight.

"It's my fault," I said quickly. "I did the measurements. I made a mistake."

The foreman sighed. "I've had enough of you lot. First Josiah disappears, then you want time off for harvest, and now this." He glared at me. "Have you lost your mind as well as your brother?"

"It won't happen again, sir," said my father, looking worried.

"You're right, it won't," answered the foreman grimly. "You're sacked."

"Both of us?" I cried in alarm. "But sir!" I searched for something that might persuade him to change his mind. "You can't sack us both. My father is the best carpenter for miles!"

"He should have noticed your error, then," snapped the foreman. But he weighed up my words. He knew I was right. "All right, Joseph. He can stay. But you're finished here."

I heard tutting and wheeled round to see the old women I'd heard gossiping before, standing just outside the building site.

One of them shook her head.

"Lazy boy," she hissed.

Anger rose in my throat, quick as vomit. I closed my eyes. "Oh, help me, Lord." Then I turned away.

I walked back to Nazareth, kicking stones and grumbling to myself. I couldn't help thinking of that day when Josiah had said all that stuff about choosing a new king. If he hadn't been fired up by that conversation, would he still have left? Maybe not. So it was all Ba's fault for going on about Bethlehem. But then it was me who raised the subject, after I heard the women talking about the census... Perhaps if I hadn't eavesdropped on them, Josiah wouldn't have left.

And I wouldn't have lost my job.

"What am I going to do now?" I muttered angrily. "What am I going to say to my mother? And Mary?"

Mary! Of course, I thought: I could get on with building the extra room ready for Mary to move in when we married. We'd got hold of the stones already; they were piled beside the house. This was the perfect opportunity to start building.

I hurried back into the village and picked up the first stones. I was feeling better already.

But I was sweaty and cross when Mary turned up, and, for the first time in my life, not pleased to see her.

We'd only been able to afford rough-hewn rocks for this wall, and they were difficult to balance and fit together.

In several hours I'd only managed to finish two layers. I was on the point of giving up.

Then Mary came round the corner.

I cursed inwardly. What would she think of me when I told her I'd lost my job? Maybe she'd go into the house without pausing to speak to me—that was what I hoped. I could talk to her later, figure out how I was going to say it. Work up to it.

But of course she didn't just go past me. She never would. She came and stood there, watching what I was doing.

I braced myself for the question: *Why are you not in Sepphoris, Joseph?*

But it didn't come.

"I wanted to talk to you," Mary said instead, her voice tight and nervous.

"Oh," I said, still nervous myself, "what about?"

"Well…" She hesitated. "I wanted to tell you… Well…"

She sighed, as though giving up on one thing and choosing another. "I was thinking about how King David didn't try to become king, it just happened to him."

"Right." I was still kneeling down and looking at my pile of stones so that I didn't have to meet her gaze. Half-heartedly I began to build again. Why was Mary so nervous if she was just talking about David? We had discussed my ancestor lots of times.

She went on. "You know the story about when God picked him out?"

Of course I know the story, I thought irritably. But I answered, "Yes. God sent Samuel, the prophet, to Bethlehem, to find a new king among the sons of Boaz's grandson Jesse."

"Yes," she said. "But when Samuel arrived, David wasn't even there. He was out minding the sheep. Because he was the least important member of the family."

Everyone knew the story. Samuel met each one of Jesse's older sons and to each of them he said no. "No, the Lord has not chosen this one... No, not this one either..." Eventually he asked Jesse, "Are these *all* the sons you have?" And someone had to go and fetch David from the hillside. When at last the boy came in (still sweaty and dirty, I bet, and much less impressive-looking than his brothers) God told Samuel that this was the next king.

"So what's your point?" I asked. My voice was impatient and I closed my eyes for a moment again, silently asking for help. I laid another stone. It fit satisfyingly in place.

"Well," said Mary, "it's... it's a good example of how God chooses humble people, isn't it? He cares about people who don't seem very important otherwise. He makes them part of his plans."

I frowned. Why was Mary talking about this? Who was she really talking about? I had no idea.

I laid another stone, and another. These didn't fit so well, but I left them there for now.

"What I mean is… Well, what I wanted to tell you… Er… the thing is, God has chosen—" Mary broke off. "Joanna!"

I stood up, looking round to see Joanna the potter's wife puffing towards us.

"Mary, it's your brother," she began.

Then there was a sudden scrape and the stone I'd just placed rolled to the ground. Or it would have done, if my foot hadn't been in the way.

"Aaargh!" I gasped, "Aaargh," and began to hop around in pain.

When I straightened up, Mary and Joanna had gone.

I didn't find out what had happened until the following day. Reuben had done something—I didn't know what—which put his father in a rage. Joanna and her husband Matthias had offered to take him with them to Judea, where they were set to travel to the next day. Somebody made the suggestion that Mary should go too and stay with her great-aunt and uncle for a few months. They spent the evening in a flurry of packing and preparations.

Then they left early in the morning, and I knew nothing about it. I was still lying in bed, thinking about that stupid wall, and wondering what on earth Mary had been trying to tell me.

CHAPTER 10

The Girl in the Herb Patch

Zechariah

I remember it well, the day Mary arrived. I had spent all morning and much of the afternoon in the synagogue. I was uneasy, not quite settled. If I could have spoken, I would have been muttering to myself, I suspect—muttering and muttering to make sense of my thoughts as I leafed through scroll after scroll and read name after name in story after story.

But then I suppose if I could have spoken, I would have been teaching lessons, not leafing through scrolls at all.

However. There I was, alone in the synagogue, not muttering. I was reading about many things. Abraham and Sarah. Jacob, Joseph. Moses, through whom God rescued all the people from slavery. Boaz and Ruth... Samuel... David... then Elijah and the great fire on the mountain. Endless stories, from generation to generation... until the last prophets spoke, and there were no new words from God anymore.

I made a note on the parchment in front of me: *Until the angel came.*

Then I paused, scratching my chin with the end of the pen. *Until the angel,* I wrote again, and underlined it.

Shouting from outside interrupted my thoughts and I stirred crossly. Since I'd come back from Jerusalem six months before, unable to say a word, the village had become chaotic with unoccupied boys who should have been learning their letters with me. Some parents set their sons to work, but others let them run around causing havoc: there had already been more than one case of stolen food and, just a few days before, my poor old cousin Thomas had been knocked flat by a stray slingshot that caught him behind the knees. Thanks be to God, he broke no bones. But perhaps those boys' next victim would.

So I hurried outside, wishing I could give them all a proper talking-to.

But when I reached the street I stopped very suddenly.

It wasn't children that had caused the shouting at all. It was soldiers.

There were two of them, muscling up the road towards me. They had thick square beards and their heads were capped with iron. They were so broad-chested they didn't seem to need any other armour—but each held a sword in his fist, a long, curved slash of sharpened metal. It wasn't often you saw swords like those in our village.

They spotted me hesitating at the synagogue door and called to me at once.

"Hey! Old man."

I drew myself up, ready to tell them to watch their tongues and be more respectful—they may have been soldiers but there were still standards to maintain—then let my breath out in a frustrated hiss as I remembered that I couldn't speak.

"We're after a young man, not from these parts," one of them said as I frowned at him. "Murdered a man in Hebron. We followed him from there. Came this way. Did you see him?"

I spread my hands to show my ignorance.

The soldier peered at me. "Someone cut your tongue out? Have you seen him or not?"

I shook my head. The second soldier swore and spat at the ground. "We've lost him now."

"No," said the first, "he'll have hidden himself somewhere." He smiled cruelly, pulling his thin lips back to reveal crooked yellow teeth. "We'll get him."

They paced away down the street. A few moments later I heard the bang of pots and the thudding of overturned tables.

Would they ransack the whole village just to find one young man? I shuddered and began to hurry home at once. Murderers! Soldiers! I didn't know which was worse. But Elizabeth was home on her own and defenceless against both.

But when I reached the house I forgot them completely. We had a visitor.

I did not recognise my niece at first. I had last seen her when she was quite a little girl, and we had had no word of her coming.

So what I saw was an unknown young woman, simply dressed, framed by the feathery green leaves of the dill and cumin plants at the edge of the herb patch. The sunlight fell on her face, which was flushed from the day's walk and upturned towards Elizabeth, who had risen to greet her.

Elizabeth cried out and clutched her swollen belly, as I had seen her do before when the child kicked or leaped within her. But there was no pain in her face. No, her forehead crinkled in amazement and her blue eyes sparkled like water.

"Blessed are you among women!" she cried in a loud voice. "Blessed is the child you will bear!"

The young woman gasped and Elizabeth moved towards her to clasp her hands. Her voice was husky with emotion: "But why am I so favoured, that the mother of my Lord should come to me?"

I froze. *The mother of the Lord?!* Six months before I would have scoffed at such words—or been angry at them. As if the Lord God could have a mother! But now… I had changed since the angel's words to me. I would not scoff. I was ready to believe even impossible things.

Elizabeth reached out a hand towards me, but she was still looking at the young woman. "The baby in my womb leaped for joy," she explained—yet she seemed more interested in the visitor's child than her own. "Blessed is she," she went on, "who has believed that the Lord would fulfil his promises to her."

What promises? What did the young woman believe? How did Elizabeth know these things? I grasped her hand in astonishment, wondering whether this was really my own familiar wife.

And Mary—for suddenly I realised who the young woman was—shone with smiles.

The song floated out from inside the house, while Elizabeth and I sat together by the herb patch.

"My soul glorifies the Lord,
and my spirit rejoices in God my Saviour,
for he has been mindful
of the humble state of his servant.

"From now on all generations will call me blessed,
for the Mighty One has done great things for me—
holy is his name."

It was our niece, singing while she unpacked her few possessions. The song was of her own invention, it appeared, and she sang it several times.

My heart beat fast to hear those words. It was true: something was happening to Mary—something even more momentous than what was happening to Elizabeth and me. "All generations will call me blessed." "The mother of the Lord." It was astonishing.

I frowned, though. She was singing about it as if it were just a private matter, a blessing from God upon just her—but if what Elizabeth had said was correct...

As if Mary could hear my thoughts, at that moment her song changed. It sounded fiercer and bolder now. It sounded like a war song. It sounded like a song that had been sung since the most ancient days.

"His mercy extends to those who fear him,
from generation to generation.

"He has performed mighty deeds with his arm;
he has scattered those who are proud in their inmost
thoughts.

"He has brought down rulers from their thrones
but has lifted up the humble.

"He has filled the hungry with good things
but has sent the rich away empty.

"He has helped his servant Israel,
remembering to be merciful

to Abraham and his descendants for ever,
just as he promised our ancestors."

Yes, I thought to myself as I sat there in the sunshine listening, *he is a God of justice. A God who rights wrongs and cares for the needy. A God who rules. And he has come himself at last.*

Yes, I thought, and I was just as astonished as I had been in the temple: the Lord God had come! And he had come wrapped not in fire, but in flesh.

He had... he had come as a child!

CHAPTER 11

Just as He Promised

Mary

Have you ever had that feeling of total, utter safety? When you just feel still and calm, like nothing can go wrong? It's like you're wrapped in five blankets at once or you're sitting by a fire hearing someone tell a really good story. Or like you're a baby in a womb.

That was how I felt while I stayed with Zechariah and Elizabeth.

Not all the time, obviously. Their village wasn't tucked away like Nazareth; it lay close to a well-trodden road leading to the capital city. So it was a busier place than I was used to. And a more uneasy one. I smiled at people every single day but they all seemed to be suspicious of me. Elizabeth said it was because of the disturbance caused by the soldiers who had been through the village on the day I arrived.

"It's the thought of that young rebel they don't like, really," she told me. "The soldiers said he was from the north, and you're from there too, and you arrived at the same time. It's not surprising they'd make the connection." She squeezed my hand. "I'm sorry, my dear."

The young murderer hadn't been found, but the villagers suspected he was still around somewhere. Food was going missing and the village children swore they weren't the culprits. So there was a sense of danger that made me feel nervous every time I stepped outside.

But within the house, it was the reverse. There was nothing at all to be nervous about. Elizabeth had known my secret without me having to tell her—and she'd said all those things in response! The miraculous child she was carrying had leaped in recognition of the miraculous child I was carrying, even though neither was yet born. My great-aunt and I had an immediate bond.

"In a way I'm glad this rebel is on the loose," she told me with a smile, "since it means I get to have you all to myself." Then she laid a hand on her pregnant belly, which grew larger all the time. "Me and this little one."

When Elizabeth said that my great-uncle wanted to take me to Hebron, the nearest town, I thought we might see Joanna and Matthias selling their pottery. I'd travelled as far as Elizabeth's house with them, but Hebron was where they had gone after that. Perhaps I'd spot them behind a market stall, and my brother slouching next to them, his fingers slicking his hair back as usual. But when we arrived I realised I had no chance. Hebron had more people in it than I'd ever seen in one place. There were cloth-sellers, leather-tanners, knife-grinders, shoemakers, food-sellers, animal-herders, tax-collectors, egg-hawkers, potters and countless others, all doing deals at the tops of their voices. Ragged boys shoved past traders in rich red robes while women gossiped at the market stalls. Soldiers swaggered on the street corners and two elderly priests pottered past us. I'd never find Reuben in a place as bustling as this.

Zechariah took me by the hand and pulled me quickly into a quieter street. Here I saw the two priests again, deep in talk, and we hurried past them and out into a wide square.

There stood the most enormous building I'd ever seen.

I mean, it was *huge*. And strong. Stone after stone reached into the sky. Each one was perfectly rectangular, perfectly smooth—and as big as me.

I thought of Joseph and the wall he'd been building the last time I saw him. There was no comparing the two.

"What is it?" I asked, gaping at my uncle. He gestured at the two priests, now coming up behind us, and cupped his ear in his hand to mime listening.

"Now this is what I invited you to Hebron to see," one of the priests was saying as they stopped to look up at the magnificent stones. "Just finished—and isn't it impressive? All King Herod's finest craftsmen were put on the job."

"And inside is—" began the other priest.

"The Cave of the Patriarchs, yes. This is where they say Abraham himself is buried, along with Sarah. And Isaac, and Jacob. The fathers of us all."

"So King Herod has built this to protect the site?" asked the second priest approvingly.

"Oh, Herod!" answered his guide with a wave of his hand. "Does he truly care for the Lord God and the history of our people? Who knows? You know he builds temples to false gods too. But I'll admit this is certainly a worthy building for such a precious place. Almost as marvellous as the temple itself, wouldn't you say? Now, let me show you..."

And they walked on.

Zechariah's eyes were crinkling in pleasure as he saw my amazement. *I knew you'd like it*, I thought he wanted to say.

I looked up again at the enormous walls.

"He has helped his servant Israel," I murmured, repeating the words of the song I'd sung the day of my arrival, "remembering to be merciful to Abraham and his descendants for ever, just as he promised our ancestors."

Those huge walls seemed like a sign: a reminder of the solidness of God's word. God promised Abraham he'd bless the world through his family, our people. He promised David that one of his descendants would rule for ever. Each promise was like a stone in an unbreakable wall. They'd never fail.

"Blessed is she who has believed that the Lord would fulfil his promises," Elizabeth had said. All my life I had believed that God would keep his promises to Abraham and the rest of our ancestors—but I had never thought that he'd make a promise specifically to me. My child was going to be the answer to the promise God made to Abraham hundreds and hundreds of years ago: "Through your offspring all nations on earth will be blessed."

I was as sure of it as those stones were sure to remain standing. My child was going to be the one. The greatest descendant of Abraham. A blessing for the whole world. I realised that my hands were cradling my belly. He was in there.

We reached the village at last. I was already thinking of my bed and the friendly silence of sleep. *I'll tell Elizabeth about the Cave of the Patriarchs and its enormous wall*, I thought happily, *and she'll kiss my head like my mother does, and we'll eat and pray and go to bed, and in the morning I won't have to walk any further than the village well.*

But suddenly my great-uncle started and broke into a run.

"What is it?" I cried. Then I saw the broken pot outside the door... the trampled patch of plants in the garden... the door, closed when it was normally open...

Something had happened.

I rushed after my uncle, my stomach feeling suddenly as empty as that broken pot. Had Elizabeth's baby come early? Had she been taken ill? Had... had that rebel youth come to steal from us?

But when I came into the house I saw Elizabeth sitting on her usual stool, looking serious but perfectly well. At her feet squatted a young man, scraping bread around a bowl of lentils.

A young man? I stopped, aghast. "The murde—!"

But Elizabeth waved a hand, laughing. "It's all right, love. Look who it is."

The young man turned around and gave me a wobbly smile.

"Josiah!" I exclaimed.

CHAPTER 12

She Cannot Hide For Ever

Zechariah

We soon found out what had happened.

The boy had indeed been hiding out not far from the village, venturing in to steal food every few days. He came to our house, he said, only because he had not been there yet; he had had no idea that Mary was staying there.

He had waited until Elizabeth came out to go to the well, and then seized his chance, running into our little courtyard to scavenge her freshly baked loaves and a handful of the figs which were drying in the sun. But as he hurried out again stuffing food into his tunic, he knocked straight into my wife, who had returned to fetch something she'd forgotten. Poor Elizabeth managed to stay on her feet, but her pot crashed to the ground and Josiah found himself sprawling among the herbs.

"Thank the Lord the baby wasn't harmed," Mary breathed as Elizabeth related this, and Josiah hung his head.

Elizabeth had taken pity on him—it was like her—and brought him inside to give him a proper meal. He needed it: his tunic hung loose on his bones and his face sagged like that of a much older man.

He told us he'd been running away not only from the soldiers I'd met, but also from the rebels he had fallen in with on the road south.

"I thought they were like me," he explained: "fighters for the kingdom, people who wanted to see a proper king on the throne again and get rid of Herod and the Romans. They told me that the people we attacked were Herod's men and the money we stole was for a good cause. But it was all a lie."

His voice was hoarse even after he had had his fill of water and food: it came out as a growl. His eyes were sunken beneath their lids. He certainly sounded and looked like a murderer. But he insisted that the soldier's claim was untrue: he had not killed anyone.

"I nearly did," he said. "I… I came close, a few times. But I never injured anyone so much that they would die. I'm sure of it."

I nodded thoughtfully. It was not difficult to decide what to do, not once Elizabeth had already taken the boy in. Taking a wax tablet, I wrote a simple message and passed it to him.

STAY HERE, it said. HIDE. DON'T GO OUT.

The poor boy almost burst into tears when he read it.

"You'll be safe here," Elizabeth said warmly, giving him another portion of lentil stew and ladling some out for me and our niece too.

And that was that.

Mary seemed pleased enough on the surface to see the brother of her betrothed. She chatted to him about his family and tried to make him laugh.

But she also seemed quieter and less sure of herself after that day.

At first I thought it was because his presence made her homesick. It was quite right that she should miss her young man, of course. His name was often on her lips, and Josiah naturally reminded her of him.

But there was something else too. Was she afraid of the boy? I had believed him when he said he was no murderer, but perhaps she feared I'd been too hasty. She was kind and polite to him, easy and friendly enough when they were talking, but I noticed her get up and walk away quickly sometimes when she heard him about to come into the room. She spent more time outside the house now, finding excuses for errands. I was sure of it.

At last my curiosity and concern were too great. I pulled Elizabeth aside and mimed my question.

I nodded at Mary and pulled a sad face. I nodded at Josiah and raised my hands in a querying gesture.

The pantomimes I had to go through in those days! But Elizabeth was good at reading my signs by now. "Why does she avoid him?" she asked, then laughed sadly. "She's afraid, Zechariah. She is pregnant, and Joseph is not the father of the baby. What will his brother do when he finds out?"

I had not thought of that, but of course Elizabeth was right. We knew that Mary was carrying a child, but there were not yet any outward signs. We also knew that the child came from God, but others would be unlikely to believe Mary's story.

Elizabeth and I stood watching our niece, whose face was concealed, her head bent over the fire as she stirred the pot. I thought of the certainty my wife had expressed on first seeing her: "Why am I so favoured, that the mother of my Lord should come to me?"

The mother of the Lord. Mary's child would be God— the same God our people had known for generations. Yet at the same time he would be a man, a servant, a son.

I did not understand how this was possible, but I believed it to be true.

If I was reading the prophets correctly, this child would suffer. He would suffer a great deal. So it was not a surprise that Mary should suffer too.

She already suffered, though it was just the ordinary hardships of a woman with child. I saw her face sometimes early in the mornings before I went to the synagogue: her forehead creased, her eyes weary. In the evenings she often went to bed early, complaining of discomfort or tiredness.

But Elizabeth was right, I knew. Mary was afraid of the greater suffering that was to come, when her pregnancy would become clear and all her friends and family would think she had done wrong.

"Perhaps we should keep her here with us," mused Elizabeth quietly. "But... she cannot hide for ever."

It was true.

I kissed my wife and went into my own room to say my prayers. I took my time about them. I had a great deal to say.

CHAPTER 13

Ruined

Joseph

I kept reminding myself how long it had been. "Two weeks since Mary left," I would say as I woke up in the morning. "Three weeks," as I went to work in my father's old workshop.

One month. I made a new door for the house of a farmer whose cow had rammed a horn through the old one.

One and a half months. I fixed a loom for one of Mary's aunts, a weaver who sold her cloth in the nearby towns.

Two months. I began work on a new table to go in the village synagogue.

By the time it was three months, I'd also made a lot of progress on the new room which Mary and I would live in when we were married. Its walls stood proudly upright; the stones fit snugly and were well plastered together. It was just waiting for a proper roof.

I admit: I was delaying. I knew I could do it—I'd built ceilings before perfectly well. But after the incident in Sepphoris... Let's just say I was nervous.

"You ought to get it done before the rains come," my mother kept going on at me. Though Josiah was still gone, she was better now—as long as nothing jogged her thoughts towards him, she seemed back to normal. (Obviously I was glad—but, I admit, I did sometimes miss the days when she hadn't nagged so much.)

I was concentrating on carving a particularly fiddly bit of decoration on a table leg one day when she came in—perfectly silently at first, so I didn't notice. Then suddenly she made her presence felt.

"Have you heard the news?"

I jumped. My knife slipped and made a deep gouge in the wood.

"Ma!" I examined the table leg carefully. No, there was no way I could disguise the cut. The design was ruined. I'd have to start again.

Sighing, I put the knife down and turned to greet my mother properly.

She had no idea what she'd made me do. "There's to be a census," she told me excitedly. "In six months' time. We're all going to have to travel to Bethlehem."

So those old women were right, I thought.

Six months... Mary and I should be preparing to marry by then. The date hadn't yet been fixed, but we had said it would be a year after the promises were first made.

But if there was a census then we might end up staying in Bethlehem for a month or even more. Which might mean delaying the wedding.

Ma seemed to read my mind. "I was thinking," she said, "—we'll see what your Ba thinks of course, and Mary's family—but maybe we could bring the wedding forward. Celebrate it before we go. It'd be a good thing for Mary to see Bethlehem."

"Yes," I answered thoughtfully, my mind immediately going to Judea and its unfamiliar hills. Perhaps Mary had visited Bethlehem already. How far away from the city did Elizabeth and Zechariah live? I had no idea.

"The city of David, you know," my mother was saying, bringing me back out of my thoughts. "City of your ancestors. It would be good for her to really appreciate what family she's joining."

I smiled. To my parents, family pride was the most important thing in the world.

But I did think bringing the wedding forward was a good idea. We could marry in the winter once the rains were over. Then take the trip south together. It would be our first joint adventure.

But nothing could be agreed until Mary was back.

The olive harvest was well over by now and we were coming to a time of festivals. We all thought Mary and the other travellers would return by the Day of Trumpets—only days away. I was so looking forward to seeing her. I expected her every day.

But when she finally came, all my hopes were torn in tatters.

I didn't realise the truth at first. She came into the workshop the morning after she arrived, still tired from the long journey but cheerful and full of things to tell me.

"I've seen Josiah," she chattered, "he's safe with my great-aunt and uncle—they're hiding him from the soldiers and—"

"The soldiers?"

"Oh I'm sorry, yes, they were chasing him and they said that he'd killed somebody but it wasn't true—and Joseph, we went to Hebron where Abraham and Sarah are buried and it was the most amazing thing—and Elizabeth was so wonderful to me, and when I arrived she..."

Mary trailed off. One hand went to her stomach and her face turned a little grey.

I rushed to bring her a stool. "Are you sick? What's the matter?"

She shook her head.

Just then my mother poked her head in. "You're back!" she cried, and Mary rose again to accept her embrace.

"You've put on weight," said my mother approvingly. "Now, when did you arrive? What news of your great-aunt?"

But Mary was looking even greyer now. She pressed her hand to her stomach again. "I'm sorry, I think I'm going to be—"

She lurched out of the room. We heard her spew her breakfast—and possibly also the previous night's dinner—onto the ground.

I expected Ma to go and help her, but instead she looked at me sharply.

"Sick…" she said, "and fatter than when she went away. Joseph, how many months is it she's been gone?"

"Three and a half," I answered, mystified.

"Hmm." She got up to follow Mary. I heard them speak to each other, too quietly for me to make out the words. Then…

I couldn't believe it.

Was that a smack I'd heard?

I rushed out. Yes. *My mother had slapped Mary in the face.* Mary was sobbing on the ground, my mother standing over her with a grim expression. Her hand was still raised.

"Ma!" I pushed past her to help Mary up. But Mary said nothing. She just hid her face from me and then stumbled away.

"Ma," I said again, "what—?"

"She's pregnant," said my mother grimly. "Three or four months gone, I'd say."

"Three…" I gaped at her.

"Are you the father, Joseph?"

I gaped again.

My mother snorted in disgust and stalked off home.

My life was ruined.

It was like my mother had taken a knife to all my hopes and dreams and gouged a huge deep line. Right through the middle.

I sat flat on the floor in disbelief.

Mary was going to have a child, and it was nothing to do with me. That meant she had lied to me. She didn't love me as much as she said she did.

I had never felt so much pain. Mary! Mary! How could she *do* this? How could she break my trust like this? How long had she been lying to me? Had all that time I'd spent with her—all that time I'd spent just *thinking* of her—had it all been a waste?

A tiny part of me—just a tiny part—did cry out that surely there must be some misunderstanding. This was *Mary*, whom I'd known all my life. Mary, who was good and true and loyal and kind. Mary couldn't be so faithless. There had to be some explanation.

Yet the facts seemed plain. Mary was pregnant. I wasn't the father of her baby. Therefore, Mary was unfaithful.

Which meant I couldn't marry her.

CHAPTER 14

Very, Very Angry

Mary

"The people of Israel were trembling with fear," I said. "They'd been in the wilderness for months now."

I was telling Abigail and Nathan the story of how our people became God's people—of how he had rescued the descendants of Abraham from slavery in Egypt, all those centuries ago, and brought them into their own land.

We would tell the story properly in a few weeks' time, during the Feast of Tabernacles when we'd build a shelter outside to remember the shelter God gave our people in those days. But there was no harm in telling it now, too. In fact it did a lot of good—to me at least. It was good to think about something other than the baby, and Joseph. And Joseph's ma.

"God had defeated the Egyptians," I said, "and allowed the Israelites to escape. He showed them the way, gave them food and made salty water drinkable so they wouldn't get thirsty. There was miracle after miracle. But the people were still afraid."

"Stupid," shouted Nathan.

"But the wilderness was *horrible!*" Abigail pointed out. She shivered. "I would've been scared too."

"He gave them fire from heaven," retorted Nathan. "And bread from the sky."

"And," I added, "he told them that they were his people, and he was their God."

"And he promised them a new place to live," said my brother.

"That's right."

Abigail pursed her lips, not wanting Nathan to have it all his own way. "But they didn't get there for ages."

I nodded. "Shall I tell you why?"

I put down the palm fronds I was twisting into a braid (we were making decorations ready for the Feast of Tabernacles) and stretched out my legs. I never seemed to be able to get comfy anymore.

"They had reached a mountain called Sinai," I began. "Moses, who was the leader, went up to the top, where God spoke to him. The rest of the people stayed at the bottom. They watched and waited for Moses to return."

"They just stood there looking at the mountain?" asked Nathan quizzically.

"Well," I said, "no, I don't know how long they actually stood there looking. I guess they had other things to do. But they did stay at the bottom of the mountain. They stayed there for a really long time."

"How long?"

"Moses was gone for forty days and forty nights. And during that time all they could see was a glinting fire far away on the top of the mountain. Everything was silent, and they were afraid."

"Afraid of God?"

"Afraid that God wasn't there and Moses had disappeared and they were on their own."

Nathan scoffed. But his eyes were round and the long palm leaves he'd been plaiting lay forgotten.

"So they decided to make their own god."

"What?!"

"They gathered up all the gold and jewellery they had and they melted it down. Then they took clay and made an enormous mould. Then they poured the gold into the mould and left it to cool, and in the morning they broke the clay to reveal a shining golden calf."

"A calf," said Nathan disbelievingly.

"A baby cow," Abigail told him.

He glared. "I know!"

"Then they told each other that the calf was a god and that it had rescued them out of Egypt."

I paused.

Nathan muttered that this was stupid.

"Yes," I said, "but it wasn't just stupid. It was a terrible thing to do. They turned their backs on the God who loved them, and worshipped something else instead."

"They were like an unfaithful wife," Abigail said suddenly.

The world went silent and still. All I could hear was my heart. Thu-thud. Thu-thud. I stared at Abi. "*What did you say?*"

"They were like an unfaithful wife," she repeated cheerfully. "Someone who lies and cheats and loves somebody else instead of her husband."

"And…" I stuttered, "and where have you heard about unfaithful wives?"

She shrugged. "Ma."

I took a few deep breaths.

"Then what happened?" Nathan asked impatiently.

"Then," I replied, recovering, "God was very angry with them."

I couldn't help it: I immediately thought about Joseph. I had not seen him since his mother had hit me in the face. But I could imagine his anger.

As far as Joseph knew, I had betrayed his trust completely—just as the Israelites had betrayed the Lord God. How could he forgive me for that? Would he even be willing to hear me explain myself?

My mother certainly wasn't. So far, she was the only person Joseph's mother had told. I think they were hoping that Joseph might admit to being the father of the baby. If he did, we might still get married—and while that was a possibility they didn't want to disgrace me in front of the whole village.

But they were both very, very angry, and they did not have any interest at all in hearing me explain.

There was anger everywhere, it seemed, even though we were supposed to be in a season of celebration. My older brother was in big trouble again: he'd been found weaving his way around Sepphoris, wine bottle in hand, shouting insults about King Herod. I had never seen my father look more angry than when he saw Reuben being dragged into the village by the pair of soldiers who'd arrested him.

"You had a fresh start," he raged after they told him what Reuben had been doing. His face was purple and his throat clogged with anger. "Joanna was full of how well-behaved you were in Judea. I was all ready to welcome you back and start again. But you can't keep yourself out of trouble, can you?"

Then it got worse. The soldiers happened to mention that Reuben had been seen in a Roman temple, praying to a foreign god. When he heard this my father fell silent and his lips became very thin. The soldiers exchanged glances and left in a hurry.

The yelling started again immediately afterwards. "Are you a son of mine or not?" my father cried again and again. "Are you a child of Abraham or not?"

He wanted to throw Reuben out and never see him

again. But Ma persuaded him otherwise. Reuben would stay—but he was not allowed out of the house until the Day of Atonement was over. That was in eleven days' time.

"On the Day of Atonement," she said, "you will ask God for forgiveness and hope that he allows you a fresh start."

"Again," snorted my father.

But when it came to me, my mother didn't even mention the possibility of forgiveness.

I sighed, twisting the braided palm fronds between my fingers. My mother was wrong to be angry at me. But God was right to be angry at the people who made that golden calf. They had done a terrible thing. And it hadn't even been the first time they'd betrayed his trust.

Yet the Lord had not stayed angry for ever.

"After that, God told the Israelites once again that they would be his people and he would be their God," I told Nathan and Abigail. "He didn't let them go to the land he'd promised them straight away, but he did keep on providing what they needed. And eventually his people made it to their new home."

"I wouldn't have forgiven them," said Nathan archly. "They didn't deserve it."

"No," I agreed. "But that's why it's a good thing you're not God."

I stood up. "Festival season starts tomorrow," I said

in my most cheerful voice. "The Day of Trumpets first, and then the Day of Atonement…"

"And then Tabernacles!" they shouted in unison.

They rushed inside, full of excitement. I grinned after them.

But when they'd gone, the smile left my face. It felt like someone had blown out a lamp, and I was alone in the dark. Thu-thud, went my heart. Thu-thud. It sounded like anger and pain.

CHAPTER 15

Announcing the Dawn

Zechariah

It was still dark and everything was silent as I stepped outside into the morning, early on the Day of Trumpets. Was I the only creature awake? No—a rat scurried guiltily along the side of the street, towards the synagogue.

I followed it. Soon I was drawing aside the bolts in the heavy door and tiptoeing into the synagogue hall where all the village would gather later in the day. The lamp flicked my shadow high onto the bare walls.

I went to a shelf and took down the long, narrow box of polished walnut wood in which we kept the trumpet. I drew off the lid and there it was, swaddled in lamb's wool: a long, twisted horn, shining and smooth after decades of careful use. I felt the weight of it in my hands for a moment. Then I set off, heading for the highest point of the village.

I could see the dark hills rippling away in every direction, their colours just visible beneath the lightening sky. I stood looking east, my breath still heavy from the walk, waiting for the sun.

Then, there it was: a blaze of orange rearing above the horizon, sudden and fierce as a stamping horse. I put the trumpet to my lips and blew. The sound was long and deep and it filled the air. Other horns answered from the nearest villages.

It was the Day of Trumpets, and the dawn had come.

I was making my way slowly back down the hill when I saw Josiah flurrying towards me.

"Zechariah!" he was shouting. "Zechariah!"

I flapped my hands at him, alarmed. Had we kept him hidden and safe for so long, all for nothing?

But he would not be shushed. "Zechariah!" he yelled again, still at the top of his voice even though he was now only a few steps away. "It's Elizabeth! She's screaming and screaming! It's—it's terrible!"

The poor boy's eyes were very wide. "I think she's about to give birth!"

The Day of Trumpets was the first of the autumn festivals, which was a time of new beginnings: a very good time to be born. In two weeks we would celebrate Tabernacles, remembering the time when our ancestors left Egypt and started their new life as the people of God.

Before that would come the Day of Atonement, when we would all ask God for forgiveness and gain our own new start. The blowing of the horn on the Day of Trumpets announced that all this was to come. We all felt it was a good day to begin life.

And our baby boy was like a trumpet himself. He yelled and yelled. If he could have talked, I think he would have had a lot to say.

On the eighth day came the naming ceremony. Our friends, neighbours and a few family members gathered: all of them eager to see this miraculous baby, born to a man and woman who were too old to have children.

"As you know," Elizabeth told them, "my husband is unable to speak. But we have already decided what the boy's name will be."

"Will you name him after his father?" one neighbour asked enthusiastically. "Zechariah is a lovely name."

"No," answered Elizabeth. I was grateful that she managed not to pull a face.

"Another family name, then," said someone else. "What was your father called?"

"No," answered Elizabeth, "it will not be a family name."

"Then what—"

"He is to be called John." The name the angel had instructed me to give him.

There was a great shaking of heads. "But there is no one among your relatives who has that name!" old Thomas told her disbelievingly. "Zechariah—that's a much better name. Let's call him Zechariah."

But Elizabeth was quite determined.

Eventually they appealed to me. "Surely you won't put up with this. What do you want him to be called?" They gestured to me as if I were deaf as well as dumb, pointing at the baby and at me and miming writing.

I sighed and copied their gestures, nodding at the tablet that lay in the corner of the room. They passed it over and watched eagerly as I put the stylus to its waxen surface.

HIS NAME IS... I wrote.

"Zechariah," someone muttered again. "Zechariah is a good name."

JOHN, I wrote.

HIS NAME IS JOHN. I held up the tablet so they could all see.

And suddenly I felt words spill onto my tongue for the first time in nine months.

"His name is John!" I cried, and they all leaped back in astonishment. With a laugh of delight I began to bellow it at the top of my newly regained voice: "His name is John! His name is John! Praise be to the Lord, the God of Israel! His name is John!"

I picked up the baby and cradled him in my arms, kissing his head before opening my mouth again to speak. I could not stop the flow of words. How can I explain it? The *sound* came from me but the source of it—the meaning of the words and the utter certainty behind them—came from somewhere else. Or someone else. I was a trumpet and someone was blowing me.

I spoke about Abraham and David and the promises God had made to our people. I spoke about how God had come to us and would walk among us. I spoke of how he would rescue us.

Did I mean he would rescue us from Herod? From the Romans? From our own wickedness, perhaps? I wasn't sure. But I knew there would be a rescue.

"And you, my child," I went on, stroking John's tiny, crumpled cheek, "will be called a prophet of the Most High."

Our neighbours goggled. One of them began to speak, but Elizabeth shushed her.

"For you will go on before the Lord to prepare the way for him," I went on, still filled with that strange certainty. "To give his people the knowledge of salvation through the forgiveness of their sins, because of the tender mercy of our God…"

I folded the child in my arms again. The final phrases came out as a kind of lullaby:

"The rising sun will come to us from heaven,
  to shine on those living in darkness
  and in the shadow of death,
  to guide our feet into the path of peace."

Yes! One day, my son would be like a trumpet, announcing the dawn. He would declare the arrival of the Lord himself. He would shout it out from the tops of hills to the deepest valleys. And then the sun would rise—Mary's child would come—and all darkness and sorrow would come to an end.

As I put John back in his cradle I saw Josiah's pale face appear at the door. He had been hiding in the darkness of the next room, but he had heard my words. His mouth wobbled and his cheeks showed the tracks of tears. But his eyes... his eyes were shining with hope.

CHAPTER 16

The Decision

Joseph

"Make up your mind, Joseph," my mother said.

I couldn't help it: my eyes kept going to the unroofed walls at the side of our house. It was the first day of Tabernacles and we were all outside, building the temporary shelter we'd eat and sleep in throughout the coming week. It was only a few paces from the room I had been building for me and Mary.

And Ma had caught me glancing at it again as I went past.

"You must either accept the child as your own or tell Mary you won't marry her," she went on impatiently. "But for goodness' sake, stop moping around. Make a decision."

I was staggering towards the box-like shelter, whose frame my father was still hammering together. My arms were filled with greenery, mostly long leafy branches of olive and myrtle. Wide palm leaves stuck out over my shoulders and silvery fingers of willow trailed on the ground. I dumped the lot at my father's feet, then turned to answer my mother.

"Let's just enjoy the feast," I said, "and then I'll decide. I promise I will. But let's not talk about it this week."

She hesitated, then nodded.

But as I picked up my tools to start attaching the branches to the roof of the shelter, I was thinking about it again. I couldn't stop.

Ma made it sound easy, but it wasn't. Deciding not to marry Mary would mean dragging her into disgrace—or worse. What she had done (or, what I *thought* she had done) was very, very serious. Once it was known, the punishment could be terrible. I did not want that.

But could I marry her, knowing that she was a liar? Could I lie myself and say that I was the father of her child? No! I might not want her to be disgraced—but to take the same disgrace on myself by marrying her? That did not seem like a good solution.

So what could I do?

I tried and tried to get myself to just focus on the festival. We all missed Josiah and I wanted to be an extra-good son in his absence. I wanted my mother to enjoy the holiday. But as we ate the special meals under the myrtle branches, as we recited prayers and told stories, as we played games and laughed with our neighbours, my eyes kept on sliding to that unfinished building beside the house. My mind kept on thinking about Mary.

On the fourth day of the feast, I decided I'd marry her. On the fifth day, I decided I wouldn't. On the sixth day, I changed my mind again.

But finally the seventh day of the feast came, and I knew that in the morning I would have to make my decision—and stick to it.

That evening my father recited the story of how the Israelites left Egypt and came towards the land God had promised them.

"The Lord God gave our people all that they needed," he said. "Food—" he glanced at the meal in front of us "—shelter—" he raised his hands to the green ceiling "—and the promise of a true home."

It was a speech he made every year. Even the serious way he was gazing around at us was the same. "After the people made the golden calf," he went on, "they feared that the Lord would abandon them. After all, that is what they deserved. But God said, 'My presence will go with you, and I will give you rest'."

"And so the people began to make a tent, an enormous tabernacle which was to travel with them wherever they wandered. It was a beautiful place." His gaze flicked to the beads my mother had hung up all over the shelter. "They brought their finest fabrics and richest ornaments," he told us. "They brought spices and oils and jewels and every fine thing they owned. They brought all these to the tabernacle of the Lord."

I knew the last words by heart. "Then God came to the tabernacle and his presence was there. And in this way he camped among his people."

"Praise be to the Lord, the God of Israel," my mother and I murmured, and we drained our glasses.

The thought came to me clearly as I drank: *Yes, I should forgive Mary.*

But I could not marry her. I just couldn't. I would tell her to go down to Judea again and stay with her aunt and uncle, at least until the baby was born. That way we could keep it all a secret. There would be no gossip and no reason to fear. She could get on with her life. I could try to get on with mine. Separately.

I smiled at my parents and leaned over to kiss them both on the cheek. "To a new year," I said.

"To a new year," they responded.

Where was I? What time was it? It was dark and cold and the wind rustled the leaves above my head. I stirred, rubbing my stiff limbs, trying to come to my senses. I peered around. Yes, I knew where I was: in the shelter. Yes. It was the night before the last day of the feast. That was right.

But where were my parents? Woozy and confused as I was, I could see I was alone. I sat up. A few leaves drifted onto my blanket. Outside the wind was growing louder and stronger: the shelter trembled and the beads decorating its wooden frame began to rattle.

Where were my parents? I fumbled around me, feeling only the cold earth. The shelter shook again. There was a crash and something like fingernails scraped at my face suddenly, then fell heavily onto my lap. I yelled and sprang up, then felt around again and realised it was just a fallen palm branch.

There was a flash of lightning and a roll of thunder. The beads were bashing wildly against the side of the shelter now. I tried to steady myself but there was nothing solid to hold onto—the wooden joints were straining and splintering, the whole shelter was about to collapse…

Then everything went silent.

I blinked. The shelter had vanished but there was no familiar house beyond it. There was just darkness. I could see nothing at all.

Until suddenly a figure appeared in front of me, crackling with light.

"Joseph son of David," it said, "do not be afraid to take Mary home as your wife."

It gestured, and suddenly I could see the house and the new walls I'd built beside it. The ceiling was done and the door hung open. Mary looked out, smiling.

"What is conceived in her is from the Holy Spirit," said the crackling figure. "She will give birth to a son"—suddenly Mary held a baby in her arms—"and you are to give him the name Jesus."

Jesus… It meant "God will save".

I thought of all the pain and trouble of the previous months. Josiah… my mother… Mary… all those cross words and all that anger…

The angel seemed to know what I was thinking. "He will save his people from their sins," he said. Yes: that was what we needed. I felt tears leaking out of my eyes.

Then sunlight came streaming through the leaves. I sat up again, gaping. I was back in the shelter and my mother and father were mumbling in their sleep beside me. The beads hung silently on the wall, just as they'd been arranged.

I knew what I had to do.

CHAPTER 17

Dream and Hope

Mary

He came round that morning. I had just snapped at Abigail for doing something that annoyed me—I can't even remember what it was now—and she'd gone off in tears. I sat down heavily on the flat stone a little uphill from the house.

"Urrgh," I groaned, my head in my hands. I wished Reuben hadn't snored all night. I wished Ma weren't so cross with me. I wished—well, no, I didn't wish that none of it had ever happened, but I wished it could be *easier, simpler, different…*

I was feeling so sorry for myself that I didn't even hear Joseph's footsteps.

But there he was, with a mad glint in his eyes and two bits of leaf sticking out of his hair.

"Come on," he said, "I want to show you something." And he set off through the almond trees.

No one else was about. Every family in the village was still in their tabernacles, clearing them away by now and piling up the tree branches against walls. They'd dry out in the sun and then be used on the fire later.

But as I followed Joseph to his house I saw that he hadn't piled away the branches of his family's shelter. He'd just moved them.

I caught him up just at the corner of the house and he took my hand to lead me to the side where he'd been building the extra room for us to live in. The walls were sturdy with stones and plastered mud. But the roof—the roof—

It wasn't just a big hole anymore.

It was finished. Or, sort of finished. It was a thick bristle of green.

Joseph had built me a tabernacle.

"I have prepared a place for you," said Joseph formally. "And now we can be married." He smiled shyly, looking at his feet. "Obviously I'll make a proper permanent roof first."

I stared at him. "But—"

"I know the truth," he said quickly, holding my gaze. "I had a dream."

"A dream—?"

But another voice interrupted.

"A dream," drawled my brother Reuben as he strolled around the corner of the house. "How nice."

Joseph went red.

"A lovely dream, and now it's all sorted, is that right, Joseph?" said Reuben. "My sinful sister will become your wedded wife? Well, I hope you know what you're letting yourself in for."

"Reuben—" I began, but Joseph was already speaking. "She's done nothing wrong. And yes, I am going to marry her," he said quietly. "The dream was from God. This is all his plan."

Reuben smirked. "Ok. And the census, that's his plan too, is it? Timed exactly when he wants it?"

"The census?" asked Joseph. "Have they announced—"

"Everyone has to go to the town their family comes from, to be registered. On the orders of the emperor himself. Heard of him?"

I was staring at my brother. I'd heard nothing about this. But Reuben was not stopping to explain. He smirked again. "So *you've* got to toddle off to Bethlehem"—he jabbed a finger at Joseph—"and *you*, dear sister, will now have to go with him, even in your... ahem... delicate condition."

"Have they announced when it'll be?" asked Joseph, finishing his earlier question. Now I stared at him. Did everyone know about this except me?

"Just at the time when she'll be ready to pop, apparently," answered Reuben with a cruel smile. "Still sure you want to take her? Still sure about that, ah, dream?"

Joseph bit his lip and I thought for a moment he'd change his mind. But he was only getting ready to give my brother a good glare. "We're getting married," he said, "census or no census." And he squeezed my hand.

"This doesn't mean you're forgiven," said Ma.

After that I went around feeling like someone had tied a big thick rope right around my chest and was squeezing it tighter and tighter. When you get married there is a lot to do and think about, and your mother is supposed to help you with everything and be all excited. But mine was leaving me to do it all on my own. She seemed determined to make it clear how little she thought of me now. Joseph's ma wasn't much more helpful, even though it was her family and her house I was coming into.

But my little sister was even more excited than she'd been for the Feast of Tabernacles, and that made up for it a bit. Plus Joseph was on my side, and when I was with him the rope felt less tight. He'd set up in his father's old place and turned himself into a village carpenter. I spent as much time as I could in his workshop.

"Maybe we should go to Bethlehem early," he said one day as I squinted at the shirt I was mending. "Make sure we have somewhere good to stay so you're comfortable for the birth."

"Somewhere to stay costs money, though," I replied. "The longer we're there…"

"The more it costs." He twisted his face. "If only I hadn't lost that job."

"I'm glad you did," I told him, "because it means you're here." I tried to look encouraging. "It's all right. I'm sure we'll be fine wherever we stay."

"I know," Joseph said.

But that was not the end of the subject.

"I'm worried about the journey as well," he told me the following day. "If you're nearly ready to give birth... It will be dangerous for you to travel."

"Joseph, it'll be fine," I insisted. "This is God's child. God's. Child. Nothing bad is going to happen."

"But what if it does?" His face was anguished. "What if we do something wrong and the baby dies and it's all our fault?"

There were a lot of conversations like that.

But eventually we agreed a plan. Joseph's parents would go to Bethlehem a little early. They'd go to Joseph's uncle and aunt's house and ask if we could all stay there. Joseph and I would travel more slowly and then when we arrived everything would be ready.

"We don't need to be afraid," I said to him. "Let's just enjoy getting married, all right?"

"All right," he answered.

So we did.

That day, there was enough food to feed half the village and what felt like a whole year's worth of dancing. Poor Abigail got so tired she looked in danger of falling over where she stood. Ma bundled her in her arms and took her to bed.

To my surprise, when Ma came outside again she threw her arms around me and burst into tears.

"My little girl," she said through the sobs. "You're going to go all the way to Bethlehem and you'll probably die on the way and I'll never see you again."

I decided to take this as a good sign and not linger on the probable-death part. "I'll come back, Ma, I promise."

"But what if you don't? And it's all been so—so—so awful!" The tears began afresh.

"It's all right," I said, although my own eyes were filling up too now. What my mother had just said was almost an apology. "It's all right."

When she let me go I took a huge gulp of fresh air. My lungs and my heart both felt as big as the sky. The world was… well, it felt newborn. It had hope in it again.

Then Joseph grabbed my hand and whirled me into another dance.

CHAPTER 18

Straightforward

Joseph

The whole world was on the move. That's what it felt like, anyway. The road was clogged with travellers, most of them heading south into Judea. Wealthy widows with sweeping robes watched over by silent slaves. Whole extended families including wizened old men and tiny twig-fingered children, all carrying their bedding on their backs. Herod's officials riding to and fro making sure law and order was kept. And mixed in with these, the goatherds and craftsmen and all the other travellers who make up the usual traffic.

"It's amazing that so many people live so far from their families," said Mary, gazing around one evening as darkness fell and campfires began to flicker everywhere around us. "I wonder if the emperor knew his census would cause this much movement."

I shrugged as I poked our own fire with a stick. "He probably doesn't care."

"No," she agreed, breaking up a little cake in her fingers and handing it to the skinny children who'd crept up to her side. "No story today," she told them: "it's late, we should all be asleep soon. But take this."

I watched her watching them go. "You can't give them all our food."

"No," she said again, "but I wish I could give them more. I thought we were poor, but *them...*"

It was true. And we were especially lucky in that, unlike so many travellers, we had a donkey to carry our things. My parents had taken Boaz but Joanna, who had a soft spot for Mary, had offered us her animal, Jakin. He was old and walked slowly, but having him made the journey a lot easier than it could have been. Plus Mary's ma felt so bad for spending all those months barely speaking to her daughter that she insisted on giving us all the food we'd need for the journey.

So all we had to do was hold Jakin's lead-rope and trudge along. We'd be in Bethlehem within a couple of weeks and when we got there we'd find my parents and they'd show us where we were staying. Mary would give birth and we'd just stay put for six weeks or so. We'd head to Jerusalem to make an offering in the temple for the birth. Then we'd go home, and life in Nazareth would begin again as normal. Just with a baby.

Straightforward.

In a way it seemed *too* straightforward. Mary told me I was fretting for no reason, but I couldn't help thinking that something was going to go wrong.

One thing was food. I was starting to get tempted to hide some of it from Mary so she couldn't give it all away. In Bethlehem we could buy more, it was true—and hopefully we wouldn't have to because we'd be staying with my uncle. But what if something did happen, what if the plan went wrong? Mary was very pregnant and it was my job to look after her. But she seemed to think it was her job to look after everyone else.

"The city of David!" she told the children who'd clustered round her as usual, on the day we came into sight of it at last. "This is where King David grew up." She swept her hand around at the hills. "And this is where he kept his sheep, probably. Imagine that! A shepherd becoming king!"

"Shepherds stink," said one of the boys, wrinkling his nose.

"When Herod dies," said another confidently, "we can make our own—"

"Sssssh!" hissed his older sister angrily. "Ba said it's a secret."

"But—"

"We're not supposed to talk about it," the girl snapped.

Mary looked at me. "Er…"

"Better not," I muttered. "Better not to know."

The little boy was puckering up his face to cry. I jumped forwards and swung him up onto my shoulders. "And do you know why it happened?" I cried while he squealed in shocked delight. "David became king because God wanted him to. And whatever God says will happen, happens."

"Yes," affirmed Mary, looking more confident. "You see, there was one time…"

And she launched into another story.

I smiled as I gripped the little boy's legs dangling over my shoulders. I liked having him there. It made me look forward to our own boy—our own baby, who we'd watch grow up. I could swing him on my shoulders and teach him carpentry and tell him stories of all that God had done. I'd be a proper father, and he'd be my son.

The future held so many unknown things—I knew that. Jesus was not going to be an ordinary child. But he *would* still be a child; our own little boy, a boy just like this one. There was no reason why any more strange or unhappy things should happen—at least not until he was grown up.

The city was ahead of us. I could see the strong walls around it and a crowd of men sitting beside the gate. A hundred stories flashed through my mind—stories about David, stories about my own father, stories of all the things that had been done and said in this city.

"Joseph son of David," the angel had called me in that

dream. Ever since, I'd been longing to go to Bethlehem. This was the city of my ancestors. I was coming home.

There is no reason, I told myself firmly, *why things should not be straightforward from now on.*

"Stop."

The man at the gate was tall and burly and he looked like he meant business. He was glaring at us. "Where have you come from?"

"Galilee," answered Mary cheerfully.

His nostrils flared, apparently in disgust. "Where exactly?"

"Nazareth," I told him. "It's a small village, just south of Sepphoris—"

"Sepphoris?" His eyebrows went up. Turning, he made a sign to another man—even taller and burlier—who was slouching against the wall. This second man straightened up and smiled at us slowly. It was not a friendly smile.

"Full of rebels, Sepphoris," said the first man, taking a step towards us. His chest was very broad. Out of the corner of my eye I saw that a club had appeared in the hands of the man by the wall. It had nails embedded in it.

I gulped.

"We're just visiting family," said Mary in a higher-than-usual voice. "For the census…"

He gave another grunt. "Family name?"

"My uncle's name is Ram, son of Matthan," I told him. "The carpenter. He has lived in Bethlehem all his life."

"Hmmm." To my relief, this seemed to be a sound of approval. The second man settled back against the wall, scowling. His club knocked against the stones. I could see holes and dents where he'd bashed it there before. And were those bloodstains?

"All right," said the first man grudgingly, "you can come in." And he turned to the next unfortunate group of travellers.

Mary and I looked at each other. Her mouth dragged a little at the corners; I could see she was unnerved. I squared my shoulders. "Come on, then. We're here!" And I pulled Jakin forwards.

CHAPTER 19

Nowhere

Joseph

"**I**t's bad news, I'm afraid, son," said Ba quietly.

We were standing in the marketplace. He'd greeted Mary with a touch on the arm and handed her a cake of dried figs to eat. "You're tired—you should sit down," he'd said, then pulled me away a few paces.

She *was* tired, I could see—more tired than I'd realised. The baby was heavy inside her now. She was stooping with the weight of him. The birth would be any day.

But my father looked almost as haggard.

"There's nowhere for you to stay," he told me.

What? "Nowhere? But what about Uncle Ram?"

He shook his head. "He heard rumours about your brother. People are saying Josiah is a murderer—that he's hiding out somewhere—they're making him out to be some big important rebel." He laughed bitterly. "Josiah! And your uncle has heard about..." he hesitated, his gaze flicking to Mary— "well, er, they don't want us, anyway. All too much trouble, Ram said. These are uncertain times."

"Uncertain times!" I said. "But Ba…" I gestured to Mary, who was already on her fourth fig. She was shifting around uncomfortably, one hand rubbing her huge belly. "As far as I'm concerned there is one *very important* certainty," I told my father, "which is that Mary's going to give birth soon."

"I know," he said unhappily. "I'm sorry, son. It's not just the census, you see, it's the fact that it's Passover next month. It's a big festival, you know, it has to be taken seriously… Ram has a big household, he can't afford food for extra guests… Lamb isn't cheap, after all." He stuttered into silence, looking unhappy. "I wish there were something I could do."

I couldn't believe it. Were they just going to abandon us? How were we going to find somewhere to stay in a strange city? I'd hardly ever even been further than Sepphoris before! And Mary was in no state to wander around endlessly knocking on doors.

"Where are you staying?" It was all I could think of to ask.

He wrung his hands. "We've found a little place… but it's expensive and there's no more room. Honestly, Joseph, you'd be better off somewhere else. You need somewhere more comfortable, more permanent. Your ma says the same."

"But you haven't managed to find us anywhere?" I ground my teeth. "How long have you been here for?"

"It's been difficult," he answered sheepishly. "Everywhere is full. But I'm sure," he added more brightly, "when people see Mary, they'll find space. They'll take pity on her."

He looked round at her, and she gave us a wobbly smile. Then he patted me on the arm. "Good luck, son." And he walked away.

Knock, knock, knock. "Any space? We've come for the census and my wife is—"

"Sorry," said the woman at the door. "Not here."

Knock, knock, knock. "My wife is pregnant," I began. "We need a—"

"No room here," scowled the man who'd answered.

Knock, knock, knock. "Please, will you give us a room?"

"What do you take me for?" screeched the apron-clad woman who lived in this latest house. "We're not an inn!" And she slammed the door shut.

Mary gave a little moan. She'd given up walking now and was sitting on the donkey, tight-lipped, pale-faced. She looked even more miserable than I felt.

"Let's try my uncle again," I said.

"He'll just say no," she muttered. But she didn't argue as I led Jakin back the way we'd come.

I had fond memories of my uncle Ram's visits when I was a child: of me and Josiah chasing him round the fields and up trees and bashing him with the little toy swords he'd made us. But the uncle who Mary and I had found in Bethlehem seemed like a different man altogether. His cheeks weren't rosy anymore; they were creased and pitted like a peach gone bad. And his eyes were as hard as stone.

"Word is you travelled here with a bunch of known rebels," he had said to me when we'd tried his house earlier that day, "and with your brother being what he is I'm surprised at you, Joseph. No—" he held up a hand to forestall me—"I'm not accusing you yourself. But you need to be more careful. Everyone knows Sepphoris is bursting with plots against the king. You're an idiot if you haven't noticed."

He paused and wet his lips, ready for another attack. "And that woman, Joseph—perhaps if you didn't have her with you we'd let you in, but really..."

"She's my wife!" I spluttered angrily, glad that Mary was out of earshot.

"Exactly," he countered. "By marrying her you've shamed us all. My family and I want nothing to do with you."

So yes, Mary was right: he had been pretty clear. But after several hours of fruitless door-knocking, I was desperate. Surely it was worth trying again. And I had a new idea of how I might persuade him.

"PLEASE!" I cried as my uncle's wife pulled the door open for the second time, "LISTEN TO ME!"

She hesitated.

"Our family takes its line from King David himself," I gabbled, "and before David there was his great-grandfather Boaz. WHO MARRIED RUTH."

I was breathing heavily. "Ruth was a foreigner and had nothing to do with anything. She wasn't part of our people. She was an enemy, practically." I held up my hands. "You know this story! Why should she have been accepted? Yet she found a place among God's people. She was welcomed—here—in Bethlehem—in your city—by your husband's ancestor. And the Lord God looked on her with favour and she had a son, and he had a son, and he was Jesse the father of David. And David became God's king."

My uncle's wife was staring at me, her mouth open.

"My wife," I breathed, "is very heavily pregnant and we need somewhere to stay. I beg you: be like Boaz. Be like the Lord God himself. Be kind to us. Give us a place."

"Look," she said weakly, but then my uncle barrelled up behind her and I knew there was no hope.

"How dare you come back here?" he said. "Get out. Now."

I had no choice. I stood back. The door slammed shut and I heard the bolts thud into their sockets.

I pressed my forehead into the wood. "Please, Lord," I muttered. "Please, please, please."

Then I heard a voice. It came from the other end of the street.

"We've got room," it said. "If you don't mind the cow."

I turned in the direction of the voice. Then I heard Mary begin to yell.

CHAPTER 20

A Tiny Human

Mary

Don't worry, I won't give you a blow-by-blow account of the birth.

It's probably enough just to say that it lasted a long time and it was very painful and there was more than one point when I genuinely thought I would die. Joseph was possibly even more terrified than I was. Meanwhile Jakin stamped his feet and the mangy cow whose room we were sharing kept mooing and mooing as if she was the one giving birth. It was horrible.

But at last, at long last, there he was: Jesus. He lay in my arms, a few hours old, wrapped up in some rags one of the women from the inn next door had reluctantly surrendered to Joseph. His eyes were like liquid and his skin seemed as soft and fragile as almond blossom. He had tiny fingers which brushed against mine. He was puffy and wrinkled and red, but he was the most perfect thing I had ever seen in my whole life.

"I half expect him to start glowing," said Joseph in a whisper.

Later, as I lay on the straw sacks that were the closest thing we had to a bed, I could hear women singing and gossiping in the street, soldiers shouting, children playing. Jesus was sleeping at last. Joseph went out briefly to buy food; he returned some time later, saying that the city was packed to bursting and everyone was talking about their arrangements for the Passover festival in a few weeks' time.

"It's odd," he mused. "They're all so excited about the festival and so afraid because of the Romans... They don't realise that the most important thing of all has already happened."

I knew what he meant—but to be honest, at that moment I was thinking more about the terror of becoming a mother than the excitement of who Jesus was. I'd looked after plenty of babies before, of course, but it's different when it's your own. Me and Joseph were responsible for this whole tiny human all of a sudden. And he was God's promised one.

I closed my eyes, took a deep breath, tried not to panic.

Just then the old man whose tiny house we were staying in—Gaddiel, his name was—burst through the door, waving his stick in the air.

"Visitors!" he cried.

And Joseph's father poked his way hesitantly into the room.

His mother was more brisk. She started tutting as soon as she was through the door—taking in the damp walls, the uneven floor, and the bony cow who took up half the space. I picked out a few crumpled sticks of straw from the folds of the rags Jesus was wrapped in, hoping she hadn't noticed them. I smoothed back my hair nervously.

"Have you got no one to help you?" she said in an accusing tone.

"I tried to get the woman from the inn to come," Joseph told her. "She was here for the birth itself. But they're very busy…"

His ma's eyebrows shot up. She tutted again and told Joseph to bring some clean clothes and a bowl of warm water—he had to ask Gaddiel for that—then sent all three men out of the room.

When she'd helped me wash she turned her attention to the baby, unwrapping and re-wrapping him more neatly. She held him up and looked at his face very carefully.

"Hmm," she said, tightening her lips. Then she gave him back. "Jacob!" she called to her husband. "Let's go."

As she swept out, she didn't trouble to lower her voice much. "He looks nothing like him," I heard her say. "That's not my grandchild."

But Joseph's father lingered, twisting his hands together with an apologetic expression. "Well," he said, "I'm glad you're doing all right."

As he put his hand to the door there was a squelching sound behind me. The cow lifted her tail and several large brown lumps dropped to the ground. They lay there in a steaming, smelly heap.

Joseph closed his eyes.

"Er," said his father, "yes, well…" And he pulled the door shut.

Later Joseph went out again, this time to register us for the census.

"I have no idea how long this'll take," he said, biting his lip. "Will you be all right here on your own?"

He'd said very little since his parents left. I knew he must have heard his mother's parting words. Perhaps it would be good for him to have something else to concentrate on.

"You go out, I'll be fine," I told him, though my stomach felt queasy at the thought of being left alone. Inside my head a voice was shouting *I don't know what I'm doing.* But I smiled. "I'll see you later."

After several hours he still hadn't come back.

The old man gave me a bowl of thin soup just before nightfall, hovering around me anxiously as I ate. He kept glancing at the baby, who was sleeping in the pile of hay Joseph had heaped up in an old feeding trough.

"Is he coming back, your man?" he asked several times. "He'd better come back."

"I'm sure he'll be here soon," I answered, but Gaddiel kept on muttering. I wondered what he would do if Joseph *didn't* come back. He'd been kind so far—surely he wouldn't throw me and the baby out?

But of course Joseph would come back. There was no question. He would. Of course he would. He would come back. Yes.

I tried to sleep, but my mind was full of leering thugs holding sharp swords and nail-studded clubs. They were tall and broad-chested and they wanted to pull Jesus out of my arms... and then they turned to deal with Joseph... and they were raising their hands against me, too...

Eventually I dropped off properly—but then the baby started screaming and I got up to feed him, cradling him close and trying to stop myself from crying too.

"There is no rock like our God," I sang quietly, thinking how strange it was that I was saying that to *him* of all people.

But Jesus didn't seem much like a rock. After he seemed to have had enough milk, I studied his face in the pale moonlight that was seeping into our little room. He was so crumpled and so tiny and so very soft.

I couldn't help asking the question, though I did say it in a whisper: "Are you really him?"

He pursed his little lips and a few bubbles of milk dribbled out. I sighed, patted his back gently, and put him back in his pile of hay.

Then I lay there, watching the way the moonlight squeezed itself through the cracks in the walls, listening to the rustle of the animals as they slumbered in the straw, feeling the rough sackcloth prickle against my skin. Waiting.

But Joseph still didn't appear.

"This is horrible," I murmured. "This is horrible. This is horrible." My voice sounded like Abigail's after she'd been told off: a thick voice with a whimper at the edges. I squeezed my eyes closed in prayer. "Lord, *help*."

Then I heard a crash from the next room, and the old man's raised voice, ragged with sleep.

"Who are you? What are you—hey!"

The door banged open. Four men tumbled down the steps into the straw.

"He's here!" one of them said.

"We found him!" cried another.

They stood up and brushed themselves down.

"We've come to see the baby," they said.

CHAPTER 21

The Skies Shone

Joseph

I was standing outside the door, hand on the rough wood, hesitating. I'd come back from the census registration and heard male voices in the room with Mary. I braced myself for danger, clenched my fists in readiness… and then heard what they were saying.

"It was the whole sky."

"Full of light!"

"And singing—"

"It was like the stars had come to life—"

"It was like God had come to earth—"

"And they said he was here—the baby—"

"The Lord himself!"

"Born to us they said! Born for us!"

So, these were not thugs.

Gently I pushed the door open. Mary was there, sitting by the manger, her face lined and puffy but her eyes bright as she looked up at the men on their knees around her. A craggy-faced older man, his hat crumpled in his excited hands. A round-faced, red-cheeked boy, too young to have a proper beard. A short man with dark skin and a torn jacket. And a fourth, the quietest, hanging back a little. His eyes kept on dragging themselves endlessly to the baby.

"We all keep sheep on the hillsides around the city," the oldest of them began—we found out afterwards that his name was Rezin. "All around—scattered quite far apart usually, but we were gathered around the fire together tonight—"

"Last night, you mean," interrupted the round-faced shepherd. "It's morning now."

"Yes," said Rezin, "of course, it's tomorrow. A new dawn…" He lapsed into silence, staring at the baby.

"So we were by the fire," the round-faced boy took up the story enthusiastically, "and watching the sheep—"

"Not that they were doing much," added the shortest of the men with a chuckle.

"No," the other conceded, "but then the fire burned low, and we were falling asleep—"

"Don't tell anyone that," said Rezin suddenly. "They're not our sheep, you know… If that got round to the owners…"

"I won't tell anyone," said Mary softly.

"Nor will I," I added, behind them.

They all jumped. I laughed. "It's all right, I'm her husband." It still felt like such an extraordinary thing to say. I folded my knees carefully, sat down beside Mary and nodded at the visitors, hoping I seemed like a proper head of a family. "Go on."

"So the fire burned low," the young shepherd continued, "and then suddenly we heard a voice!"

"A voice as old as the hills," said the fourth man.

"And it was amazing—terrifying—it was like daytime almost, the light—the whole world was transformed—"

"I thought that was it—the end. But then the voice said, 'Do not be afraid,' and I realised—I realised I wasn't dead." Rezin was still looking down at the baby in his pile of hay. His words were full of emotion. "Then the voice said, 'Today in the town of David a Saviour has been born to you.'"

"Good news, it said," added the shortest man, "that would cause great joy for all the people."

"The Lord!" whispered the round-faced shepherd. "The *Lord*!" And he too began to gaze into Jesus' face. I wondered what he was looking for. Jesus himself just slept on.

Mary was nodding eagerly. "Did you see the angel? Did he smile—did his face light up?"

I remembered my own experience of an angel. "Was there wind," I asked, "and thunder, like God himself had come?"

"Oh," said the shortest man, "it was not quite like

that… I mean, yes, but…"

He waved his hands in the air, speechless.

"The skies shone," said the fourth shepherd simply. "There were thousands and thousands of angels. Every one of them was singing."

"God's armies," said Rezin, "announcing his arrival."

"We were awake then, I can tell you," said the short man, recovering his voice. He wiped his brow. "We were awake then."

The room fell silent. Even the animals seemed to hold their breath as the shepherds paused to remember what they had seen. I tried to imagine it: a whole hillside filled with light. Terrifying.

Outside the birds were starting to sing. I heard a sparrow flutter to the ground to peck and flurry in the dust.

"What did they say?" I asked. "The angels?"

"Glory to God in the highest heaven," answered the solemn man in a low voice, "and on earth peace to those on whom his favour rests."

Jesus stirred in the hay. His eyelids puckered open to reveal his brown eyes.

"I'm sorry," said one of the shepherds softly, "we should have brought a gift."

"We just came as quickly as we could," said another.

"Do you have plans for Passover?" asked the round-faced shepherd with sudden enthusiasm. "We could bring you a lamb."

I looked at Mary. We didn't have plans, no. We'd assumed we'd celebrate Passover with my parents and my uncle—but it was clear that Ram didn't want us.

Ba had told me earlier that evening that he would try to see my uncle after the festival was over. "Once all the festivities are out of the way and everything's been done correctly, he'll be more relaxed," he had said while we waited to be registered, standing around in the middle of an endless crowd of people. "Until then let's stay out of his way."

"We should celebrate Passover," I had answered, and he had shaken his head. "It's so expensive to stay here. We can't afford a lamb too. Best just to keep our heads down, Joseph. You look after Mary and I'll look after your ma. We'll speak again after the festival is over."

So no, we had no lamb for the Passover meal. We had nothing, really. Just Gaddiel and Jakin and this tiny room full of straw and cow dung.

"We can bring you a lamb," repeated the shortest shepherd. "We'll put our money together. It's the least we can do." They were all nodding.

"And," Rezin said, his voice cracking a little, "for now, just for now, can we stay here?" He looked up and I saw a lined and weathered face: a creased forehead, rough cheeks, a terse grey beard on his chin. But his eyes were full of emotion as his broad finger brushed the baby's forehead. "Just for a little while?"

CHAPTER 22

Like the Lamb

Mary

"A very long time ago," I said, "the descendants of Abraham needed a saviour.

"They were trapped in Egypt as slaves, building cities for Pharaoh or labouring in the fields around the waters of the Nile. They worked all hours under the skin-cracking sun and the blistering whips of the slave-drivers."

We were telling the Passover story together, me and Joseph and Gaddiel. We were in the main room of the old man's little house, which was a bit bigger and a bit cleaner than the one with the cow. (Only a bit, though.) The delicious smell of roast lamb was rising from the fire and I was trying to ignore the eager growling in my stomach.

"And then the worst thing of all happened," I went on. "Pharaoh, the king of the Egyptians, gave this order to all his people: 'Every boy that is born among the Israelites you must throw into the Nile.'"

Every single baby boy! I paused—I couldn't help myself—and looked down at Jesus. I sneaked my finger into his little fist and he squeezed it. I shook my head. How could anyone bear to kill a little child?

But they did.

"The Egyptians went snarling into the houses of the Israelites and began to tear babies from their mothers' arms. The river was filled with the blood of the children of Abraham, and the houses of the Israelites rang out with wailing. They were crying out in pain."

"And begging God to rescue them," added Joseph quietly.

There was silence for a moment. Then Gaddiel said, "And the Lord God heard their cry."

"In time," I nodded, "God spoke to a man named Moses and told him that he was to lead his people out of Egypt into the land which God himself had promised them—the same land he had promised to Abraham many generations before. A land where they would be free."

"Moses gave Pharaoh many warnings," said Gaddiel. "God sent plague after plague, and each time Moses passed on God's command: 'Let my people go!' But Pharaoh would not listen. His heart was hard."

Gaddiel got up unsteadily and I handed him the bowl of lamb's blood and a bundle of twigs. Stepping over Joseph, he leaned on the doorframe and began to fumble with the latch.

"At last," he went on, his voice quivering, "God said,

'I will bring one more plague on Pharaoh and on Egypt. Every firstborn son in Egypt will die.' And he told the children of Abraham to kill a lamb and daub its blood on the doorposts. It would die in the place of their own sons. It would be a sign that they were God's own people, and it would rescue them from death."

He opened the door and stood on the threshold, dipping the bundle of twigs in the thick blood, then scraping them against the doorframe.

"The angel of death did not enter the houses where blood had been painted on the door. But every other house, he did enter. And so now it was the houses of the Egyptians that were filled with wailing. But the houses of the Israelites were busy with preparations for the journey out of slavery."

Joseph steadied our host's arm as he sat down again. "Careful."

The two of them began to pull pieces of lamb out of the clay oven.

"With that lamb, God saved his people," Joseph said, finishing the story while the old man settled himself back onto his low stool. "He brought them out of Egypt and he camped among them as their God. And the people were God's own people, and they lived in the land God had given them. Which we do to this day."

He began to hand out the meat, wrapping it in pieces of warm floury flatbread. His rough hands touched mine as he gave me my portion.

"Eat and remember," he said formally.

We all munched in silence for a while. Then Gaddiel nodded at the baby. "Your firstborn son. Will you take him to the temple? Make a sacrifice for him?"

I nodded. "In a few days' time."

"An extra little celebration of Passover," said Gaddiel approvingly. "When I took my own son to the temple—years ago, you understand—it was the wrong time of year altogether. I dedicated him to the Lord all right, but it just seemed like—like empty words. I had no gratitude like you'll have, fresh from thinking of all those children killed in Egypt, and the great rescue."

He sighed. "But then it's a hard thing, if you take it seriously. To give your own child to the Lord. To say he can do whatever he wants with him."

I thought of Hannah, who gave up her son Samuel— the son she'd longed for. She promised him to the Lord just like we would promise Jesus to the Lord, and when he was still very small she took him to the temple again and left him to grow up there and serve God.

Which he did. But to be honest I'd never really thought about how painful that would have been for her.

That wasn't quite what it meant, though, nowadays, to dedicate your firstborn to God. Jesus wouldn't have to go and live in Jerusalem. He would grow up with us, in Nazareth.

But he would be special. More special than we'd even managed to imagine.

"I think God will do what he wants with your child whether you want him to or not," said Gaddiel, interrupting my thoughts. "So you'd better be ready."

"You make that sound like a bad thing," said Joseph uncomfortably. "What do we need to be ready for? This child is—he's—he's the one God promised. The Saviour, the Messiah, the Lord. He's going to bring peace and favour."

"The Saviour," Gaddiel repeated seriously. "Like the lamb."

Like the lamb.

The heat of the rich roasted meat had been spreading through my body, but now suddenly I felt cold. I cuddled Jesus close.

"He is the Lord's," I said slowly. "You're right. He's the Lord's. We'll be ready for anything."

But in my heart I was thinking: *like the lamb?*

I realised I hadn't really asked the question before. How would Jesus rescue us? And when?

CHAPTER 23

A Stick and a Sword

Joseph

As we walked up the slope into the outer court of the temple, I saw that it was like a huge square, all paved with even slabs which echoed with the footsteps of hundreds of people. The gateways were carved with complicated patterns and made of the very best wood— wood like I'd never seen. Huge stout beams of cedar that must have been grown in the forests of the north and brought down to Jerusalem especially. Everything was on a huge scale. I felt like a tiny child or a helpless bird in a world that was too big for me. I had an urge to run laps with my hands in the air.

Mary's eyes were as round as mine, but not because of the space. She was looking ahead at the central temple building. It was cut off from us by a colonnade but it was so tall we could see much of its walls, its glinting roof, even the tops of the huge doors.

"The holy place," Mary breathed. "Joseph, I feel like we're at the centre of the world."

Then Jesus screwed up his little face and began to absolutely bawl.

That got people's attention.

There was an old woman sitting beside one of the carved pillars at the edge of the square whose head snapped round instantly. Her hooded eyes connected with mine but I couldn't tell what expression was in them: was it curiosity, irritation, fear? Her bony hand went to the stick leaning against the wall beside her. But before she could get up, Mary tugged at my arm and I looked round to see a man hurrying towards us.

He was dressed in a blue so deep it was almost black, with a prayer shawl folded neatly over his shoulders. Before I could move he had taken the baby out of Mary's arms with two shaking hands.

"Hey—" I said, but half-heartedly because—well, just because of the way he was looking at Jesus. The man's face was grizzled with age but his eyes were clear and they were filling with tears. He cradled the baby in the crook of his arm, brushing some of the tassels of his shawl over Jesus' uncovered feet so that he curled up his toes.

I had been about to cry, "What are you doing?"—but I swallowed the words, and he spoke instead.

The man looked away towards the temple building which rose into the blue sky. "Sovereign Lord," he said in a voice stronger than his body suggested it should be, "as you have promised, you may now dismiss your servant in peace." He squeezed his eyes closed for a moment. "My eyes have seen your salvation. I can now die happy."

He bent his head to kiss Jesus' forehead. "Your salvation," he repeated, still praying, "which you have prepared in the sight of all nations. A light for revelation to the Gentiles, and the glory of your people Israel."

People around us were stopping to stare. A bearded Greek trader, a woman wearing gold around her neck, a tall Arab with his even taller son in tow: they'd been walking past, occupied with their own business, but now I could feel their eyes on us. No wonder. A light to the Gentiles—that meant all the people in the world! Anyone and everyone.

The old man was so wrapped up in his own prayer that he didn't seem to notice all those listening ears. Gently he handed the baby back to Mary. "This child," he said in a clear voice, making eye contact with both of us for the first time, "is destined to cause the falling and rising of many in Israel. He will be a sign that is spoken against, so that the thoughts of many hearts will be revealed." He placed a quivering hand on Mary's head, as if she herself were a little child he was blessing. "And a sword will pierce your own soul too."

A sword will pierce your own soul too? Dread tumbled down the back of my neck. I put my arm round Mary's shoulder, but I squeezed too tight and she squirmed and shrugged me off. We looked at each other.

A few days before, when Gaddiel started talking about Jesus being like the Passover lamb, Mary had seemed just as frightened as me. We'd both avoided discussing it since then, but I'd lain awake at night worrying about it, and I thought that she had too—in between feeding Jesus whenever he woke.

But worry had never been Mary's style, and now her eyes were as clear and peaceful as the old man's.

I sucked my lips in between my teeth. *I love you, Mary*, I was about to say. *I don't want you hurt.*

But instead I just said, "OW!" There was a stick prodding my back.

It was the old woman with the hooded eyes. "Young man," she said, still jabbing at me even though I'd turned to face her, "do you know who this child is?"

"Yes," I said. "Well… yes."

It felt like there was too much to say.

"This child is the one promised," she told me. "The one who will restore this temple—" she waved the stick up and around— "this city—" she gestured over my head and I ducked to avoid the blow— "and our people."

"And," added the old man behind me in gentler tones, "the whole world."

"Simeon," the woman greeted him, nodding abruptly. "You are quite right. And now you have indeed seen the

Saviour, as the Lord promised you would. Now you can go in peace."

"Anna," bowed Simeon in answer, "praise be to God!"

"Thanks be to God, the Lord Almighty," the old woman responded, banging her stick on the stone beneath her feet. Then she looked around at the crowd that had gathered. "Are you hoping that God will keep his promises?" she cried, stumping towards them. "Well, he has! He has!"

It felt dangerous to be in Jerusalem after the old woman Anna had attracted so much attention. I kept thinking back to those children on the road: the little boy who'd started talking about a new king, and the sister who'd shushed him. Then the guards outside the gates, and my uncle's sharp voice at the door: "Word is you travelled here with a bunch of known rebels, and with your brother being what he is I'm surprised at you, Joseph. You need to be more careful."

In other words, it was a bad idea to talk too loudly about new kings. And that wasn't exactly what Anna had done—but it wouldn't be too difficult to interpret her words that way. Nor the old man's. "This child is destined to cause the falling and rising of many in Israel." I could imagine the interrogation: *the falling and rising of who, exactly?*

"Why do you keep looking behind you like that?"

complained Mary as we made our way through the city. "It's like you think we're going to get attacked."

I shook my head, not wanting to worry her. "Just looking around," I said cheerfully. "But we should get along. Sun's shining: it'll be a nice walk back to Bethlehem. We ought to go."

She frowned.

"Let's get some food first," I suggested, relenting. "What d'you fancy? We've got enough to buy something special, I think, just this once."

"Hmmm. Ok." She quickened her pace. "Is the market this way?"

I managed not to look over my shoulder again the rest of the time we spent in the city. But I was very glad when we were back on the road to Bethlehem.

CHAPTER 24

No Stars Except One

Joseph

The last set of strange visitors came in the darkest part of the night. I woke up suddenly to find them standing over me like tall rocks, their silent faces carved with slight smiles.

"Sssssh," said their leader, his finger on his amused lips. "You'll wake the baby."

Mary was next to me. She was asleep, her breathing slow and steady. Beyond her lay Jesus, also asleep.

I scrambled to a sitting position. "Who—who are you?"

"We followed the star," said one of them simply.

He scuffed at the straw with his feet, clearing a space, and sat down cross-legged, twitching the thick fabric of his robes neatly over his knees. His companions followed suit. They were as dignified as if they were in a palace. One of them produced an oil lamp and set it burning.

Then they began their story.

"We come from the east," the first of them began, leaning forwards and speaking in a low, smooth voice. "Some time ago we saw a new star rise and we sought to learn its meaning."

"We consulted many scrolls," said the man on the left, whose dark hair was covered with an embroidered cap with silver threads in it. "And we learned that this was the star of a child who would be born king of the Jews."

"We came, therefore, to worship him," said the third man simply.

"But we went astray," added the first. "We made for Jerusalem: the capital of the Jews. We rode to the palace of Herod and requested an audience."

"It is a sumptuous palace," said the man with the cap, "rivalling even the great pavilions of the east. It is a place fit for a king." He narrowed his eyes. "But our guesses were wrong."

"We half-expected to find Herod himself dead, and a child born to take his place. After all, it was said he would be born a king," the first man said. "But Herod still clings to life and to kingship. And there has been no child born in the palace."

"However, the king was pleased to see us," went on the third man. "He entertained us very grandly."

"He asked us many questions about what we had seen and read," added the leader of the three, the first one to have spoken. I noticed that he had a gold ring in one ear: it glinted in the unsteady light. "But at last he told us we must go to Bethlehem."

"There was a prophecy we had overlooked," explained the man sitting on the left. "The king's scholars drew our attention to it."

"A prophecy," added the first man, "addressed to the city of Bethlehem itself: 'Out of you will come a ruler who will shepherd my people Israel.' The new king would be born—perhaps had already been born—here in this very town!"

The three of them looked at me with an air of triumph.

I shook my head. "But Bethlehem..." I said slowly. "There are a lot of people in Bethlehem. Why are you *here*?"

For a moment they were silent again, smiling those mysterious smiles.

Then: "The star, of course," they said. "We followed the star." And they looked up as if they could see through the ceiling.

Mary stirred beside me. Her eyes were moving beneath their lids. The baby wriggled too.

I said, "The star led you to this exact house?"

They nodded. "See for yourself."

So I stood up and tiptoed out. The air was even colder outside, and the sky was absolutely black. No moon. No stars.

Except one.

I had to bend my neck right back. It was directly above me, eerily close, bright and glimmering and pure white.

I laughed aloud.

When I got back inside I found that Mary and Jesus were awake and the three visitors were on their knees, bowing deeply. That was the moment when they unwrapped their gifts.

"Gold, frankincense and myrrh," they said. The coins gleamed in the lamplight. The flask's rich scent curled into my nostrils.

"But why?" Mary was gasping. "Why have you come? You say he's the king of the Jews—but he's not *your* king. I don't even really understand how he's our king. That's what the angel told me he'd be, but right now the king of the Jews is Herod, and after Herod it'll be one of his sons, or someone else the emperor chooses. So I don't... I don't understand."

Without making a noise, the men straightened up again, sitting back comfortably in the straw as if they belonged there. They looked from Mary to me and back again, their chiselled faces very serious.

"He has been sent by your God, has he not?" said the man with the silver cap quietly. "He has been sent not just as a ruler but as a shepherd too: one who will care for his people and provide what they most need."

"To rescue us," I said. "To save us from our sins."

"Yes." The man's dark eyes flickered. "We have no king like this for our people. We have no God like this."

"We seem rich to you, perhaps," said the man with the gold earring, "but we are as poor in spirit as anyone. We know sadness and pain and anger; we face darkness and distress. What solution is there to these things?"

"But we have hope," the third and quietest of them added, "because we know that your God is a generous God. One who will be a shepherd not only to your own people but also to foreigners like us. Did not Ruth, the great-grandmother of your King David, come from an eastern land? And did she not become part of your people?"

"And did not the prophet say that this child would be a light for the nations?" added the man with the cap.

"Therefore," said the third man gravely, "we have come to worship him."

They knelt down again and bent themselves forwards, stretching out their long fingers so that they just touched the cloths Jesus was wrapped in.

Then they stood, and rearranged their robes, and were gone.

If it hadn't been for their gifts, we would have thought it had all been a dream. But there in the straw were a tall flask, a round casket and an ornately carved wooden box. Mary opened the box hesitantly and ran her fingers through the pile of gold coins. They clinked musically. They *shone*. They shone like the stars.

We looked at each other.

"He really is," I said. "He really is going to be a king."

Mary uncorked the flask, reeling a little at its heavy scent. At the same time, Jakin lifted up his head and brayed angrily, spewing hot smelly breath all over us.

I burst out laughing. "But how that is going to happen, I have no idea."

CHAPTER 25

The Road Again

Mary

I was being shaken awake. There was urgency in Joseph's voice: "Mary. Mary. We have to go. We have to go now."

"What—?" I squinted at him. "Where—is it the morning?"

"No," he said, groping around for an oil lamp, "it's still dark. But we have to leave Bethlehem now. Now."

I struggled upright, leaning over to check Jesus in the manger. He was awake, but his little eyes were screwed up as if he was afraid.

"What's happened, Joseph?"

He was packing by this point, grabbing things and thrusting them into his bag, not even looking at them, just bundling them up and shoving them in.

"Joseph." I was scared now. "Why do we have to leave? Talk to me!"

He paused and looked at me properly. He bit his lip. "I had a dream," he told me. "Another angel dream."

"The angel!" But my joy faded as I met Joseph's eyes. It seemed like the angel hadn't brought good news this time.

"He said King Herod is searching for Jesus." Joseph's voice was flat. "He wants to kill him."

"WHAT?" Ice-cold fingers raked down my spine.

"The easterners went to him first, didn't they?" Joseph said grimly, starting to pack again. He attacked his blankets, getting them all rucked up so they rolled into a floppy spiral. "So that's how he knows. And he feels threatened."

"Let me," I said, reaching for the blankets. "You're in too much of a hurry."

"Don't you get it, Mary?" he hissed. "We are in a hurry! We need to be in a hurry! Herod's men could be outside right now for all we know! The easterners might have told them where we are!"

"I'm sure they wouldn't—"

"They probably don't know that Herod wants to kill him! They told us he said he was really interested! They probably think he wants to come and *adopt* Jesus or something!"

It began to sink in. Trying to stay calm, I pulled the blankets away from Joseph, unrolled them, smoothed them out, and re-rolled them more carefully. "So where are we going to go?"

"Egypt." He didn't meet my eye.

"Egypt!" I put down the blankets. "Egypt! But Joseph—"

"I know," he cut me short, "Egypt is the wrong direction. We'll be going further away from home. But that's what the angel said. And Mary, we can't risk going back to Nazareth. We won't be safe. We have to leave Herod's lands completely."

I pulled Jesus out of the hay, cuddling him to myself, feeling the comfort of his solid, warm flesh. "When will we be able to come back?" I whispered.

But Joseph just shook his head. "Who knows?"

We were trying to be as quiet as we could. We had no idea when Herod's orders had been sent out: it could be that soldiers were already prowling the city looking for baby boys. If the guards at the city gate knew about it, we'd be in trouble.

"Our God is a rock," I whispered, stroking the hair of Jesus' head, praying that he wouldn't wail and give us away. We peered forwards. Yes: there were dark figures by the wall—big ones. They stood on either side of the gate, looking out towards the road. There were torches set on the walls above them, their flames flicking weird shapes onto the stone. Too late, I realised that behind Joseph loomed a huge shadow. The bags on his back made it giant and misshapen—and very obvious.

There was a rasp of metal as one of the guards drew his sword. "Hey! Who's there?"

Joseph stood very still.

Footsteps came towards us. Heavy ones. I heard the smack of wood against a man's broad palm. That club... I shrank into the shadows.

"Show yourself!" The guard's voice was like a rasp of iron. "No one is to leave or enter this town tonight. No one. On the orders of King Herod himself. Now, step into the light where we can see you."

We were too late.

We were trapped.

It was all over.

I breathed in very slowly, trying not to let my chest judder with fear. Joseph still stood motionless.

Then—"Please, I'm just a traveller, nobody, nothing, I'm nothing to bother about—"

The reedy voice came from the direction of the road, on the other side of the gate. It wasn't us the guards had seen at all. It was some other poor traveller. Someone coming into the city.

"Who are you, then?" barked one of the guards.

"And what do you want in Bethlehem?"

Their voices weren't so close now. The torchlight flared suddenly and I could see the soldiers' lumpen backs, turned away from us, and the pale face of the man they were interrogating. The poor man looked terrified. I wondered who he was.

I felt Joseph tug my sleeve. "Come on," he hissed, pulling me away. We pressed ourselves to the wall where the shadows might protect us. Jesus stirred and wriggled, but kept quiet. I breathed in and out, in and out, as we crept towards the gate.

And then we were through, and Joseph began to move more quickly, heading around the edge of the city, away from the guards. He trod very carefully, not making a sound. I followed, touching the huge rough stones of the city wall and squinting as I tried to see where to put my feet.

I glanced back once and saw the pale man entering Bethlehem, flanked by the two soldiers. *Will they let him alone or are they arresting him?* I wondered briefly—but then we were round the corner and Joseph began to run, the bag on his back banging up and down like a rider who couldn't keep his seat. It would have made me laugh if I hadn't been so afraid.

I stumbled after him, one hand placed protectively over Jesus' head, my breath coming out in big ragged gulps.

We'd made it out of Bethlehem.

We kept away from the road as we went south, still fearful of Herod's soldiers and anyone else who might wish us harm. Several times we had to stop to rearrange baggage or feed the baby, and all in darkness—we didn't dare so much as light a lamp. We passed endless slumbering villages and skirted the edges of restless towns.

At last we had gone so far south that we felt we could relax. We had climbed to the top of a hill, one of the last in Judea. Even in the low light before the sun rose, we could see for miles and miles. The rocky hills rolled away from us, revealing neighbouring settlements, scattered farms and green fields. To the south lay the wilderness, and in the distance the hazy horizon, where Egypt began.

The bitter smell of smoke reached our nostrils from somewhere far below. The clank of cowbells echoed through the valley. People were rising to begin the day. I fed Jesus and then rocked him to sleep.

"We should go," I murmured, but it was nice to stand there for a while and just look. I held Joseph's hand, swaying a little as I tried to keep Jesus soothed. Then I let go to shield my eyes.

The sun had risen: its steady light shone orange on the rocks and trees and all the valleys and hills around us, so that everything seemed to have caught fire. The shadows pulled back as the light spread, and I turned in a circle, looking south and west towards Egypt, east to the desert lands beyond the Jordan, then north towards Bethlehem and Jerusalem. Beyond them were Galilee, with Nazareth and Sepphoris and everything else in our old lives—and further on, Syria and Cilicia and countless other lands. Places I'd heard of and places I'd never heard of. All lit by the same sun.

"The light's come," I said to Joseph quietly.

He put his arm around me. "We've got a long way to go."

Notes

I f you're wondering which bits of *The Promise and the Light* we know for certain and which bits I've invented, you've come to the right place. These notes explain some of the decisions I made and point you to the Bible passages which contain the original accounts.

What do we know for certain? Lots of things. We know that the first Christmas happened during the time when Herod, known as "the Great", was king of the Jews—under the overall rule of the Roman Emperor. We know that an angel appeared to a priest called Zechariah while he served in the temple in Jerusalem, and told him that his wife Elizabeth would give birth to a son; and that the same angel appeared to a young woman called Mary, six months later, with similar news. We know that Zechariah lived in Judea, in the hills around Jerusalem, and that Mary lived further north, in Nazareth, in the region of Galilee. We know that Mary visited Elizabeth while the two of them were both pregnant. We know that Joseph, who was engaged to Mary, considered breaking off the marriage but changed his mind after he, too, had a visit from an angel.

Jesus was born in Bethlehem, was laid in a manger, and was visited by shepherds and wise men. King Herod heard of his birth and tried to have him killed, but Joseph was warned by an angel in a dream and escaped with Jesus and Mary to Egypt. Eventually, after Herod died, they returned to Nazareth, where Jesus spent most of his childhood. All this we know. It's in the Bible accounts.

We also know lots about that period of time more generally: what life was like, how people lived, what they ate and what events they celebrated, what they believed about God, what the laws were, and so on.

But there's lots we don't know, too. We don't know for sure exactly when the first Christmas happened (though we can make good guesses—keep reading to find out more). There's also lots of detail which the Bible writers don't tell us. So, many of the characters and events in *The Promise and the Light* are imagined: they're based on real things that could have happened, but they're not certainties.

Just so you know, I invented the following characters: Abigail, Josiah, Nathan, Reuben, Gaddiel, Joanna and Matthias the potters, Zechariah's cousin Thomas, Joseph's uncle and his wife, and (last but not least) the two donkeys, Boaz and Jakin.

WHEN DID CHRISTMAS HAPPEN?

Jesus was born on December 25th, right? And in the year 1 AD? Actually, no. Historians aren't certain exactly when it happened, but it's likely to have been a few years before that. And it probably didn't happen in December either. That date got added later. And it wasn't until five hundred years later that a man named Dionysius introduced the counting system for years that we use today. He aimed to start counting in the year that Jesus was born. He was a few years out...

The Gospels (the four accounts of Jesus' life in the Bible) tell us that Jesus was born while Herod the Great was king—and Herod died in 4 BC. That's four years before 1 AD. So Jesus could have been born that year, or any time in the few years before then.

As for the exact date—well, I don't claim to be an expert on this subject, but I had to make a choice about when Jesus would be born in my version of the story. So I chose early March. I chose this partly because winter would have been over by then, which would have made travel more straightforward. I also compared the timeline of the Christmas story with the Jewish calendar, and found that there were certain key moments that fit perfectly together if I put Jesus' birth in March.

But I might well be wrong. Nobody knows for sure when it happened. The most important thing is that it really did happen—and almost all historians do agree that Jesus definitely was a real person who lived in the first century.

PROLOGUE

Isaiah was a prophet who lived about 750 years before Jesus was born. You can read his words in the Bible in the book of Isaiah. The bit I've quoted comes from Isaiah chapter 9, verse 2.

CHAPTER ONE

Sepphoris was the closest town to Nazareth—a few miles away. It's not mentioned in the Bible but we know about it from other historical sources.

Read Luke 2 v 1-4 to find out what the Bible says about the census. You could also have a look at Matthew 1 v 1-16, which is a list of all Joseph's ancestors. Can you find any familiar names?

Other than that list, we don't know much about Joseph's family. I had fun imagining what they might have been like! Joseph might have had lots of brothers and sisters, but I chose to imagine just one. He calls his father "Ba" because in Aramaic, which is the language a poor Jewish family would have spoken, the word for "Dad" was "Abba".

Does it surprise you that Joseph is working on a building site? He's traditionally been called a carpenter (someone who works with wood), but the word that is translated "carpenter" in Matthew 13 v 55 can also just mean "builder". Historians think that more work would have been done with stone than with wood in the area around Sepphoris, so I chose to imagine

Joseph as a bit of a jack-of-all-trades—a carpenter and a builder.

CHAPTER TWO

We don't know exactly how Elizabeth and Mary were related to each other—just that they were relatives (Luke 1 v 36). Historically, they've often been called cousins, but since Mary was young (girls in the first century married when they were still teenagers) and Elizabeth was too old to have a child, I thought great-aunt and great-niece seemed more likely.

We also don't know how other people heard about Elizabeth's pregnancy. In Luke 1 v 25 she says that not having children had brought her "disgrace among the people"—which makes me think there would have been gossip when she did become pregnant! It would have been a huge surprise. I've imagined the gossip spreading from the hill country of Judea near Jerusalem (where Elizabeth and Zechariah lived—Luke 1 v 39-40) all the way to Galilee, in the north of Israel, where Joseph hears it.

Luke 1 v 5-25 tells us more about Elizabeth and Zechariah. Don't read it all yet, though, or it'll spoil chapter 4!

If you're curious about the stories of Sarah and Abraham and Hannah the mother of Samuel, you can read about them in Genesis 18 v 1-15 and 21 v 1-6 and 1 Samuel 1 v 1 – 2 v 10; but they'll also appear again in later chapters.

CHAPTER THREE

Mary's story about Abraham and Sarah comes from Genesis 18 v 1-15 and 21 v 1-6. Have a read of the story for yourself: would you tell it differently to the way Mary does?

CHAPTER FOUR

Luke 1 v 8-25 tells us about Zechariah's experience in the temple. Luke doesn't describe the angel at all, but there is a description of angels, including of their six wings, earlier in the Bible, in Isaiah 6 v 2.

CHAPTER FIVE

The story of Hannah comes from 1 Samuel 1 v 1 – 2 v 10. You would think that the books of 1 and 2 Samuel would be all about Samuel, Hannah's son—but in fact, although the story starts with him, the focus switches to the first kings of God's people—Saul and then David. Maybe that's not surprising, given that Hannah's song talked about a future king.

The Bible doesn't say anything about Mary's family—Abigail, Nathan, Reuben and their parents are all imagined.

CHAPTER SIX

The words which Joanna says to Joseph as he walks through the village come from Ruth 4 v 11, where the people of Bethlehem pray for the marriage of Boaz and

Ruth. The book of Ruth is only a few chapters long and it's well worth a read. Remember, Boaz was a descendant of Abraham and the great-grandfather of King David. So he was Joseph's ancestor too.

CHAPTER SEVEN

Zechariah's story about Ahab and Elijah comes from 1 Kings 18 v 16-46.

Several centuries after Elijah (but still several hundred years before Zechariah), God told the prophet Malachi that he would send someone like Elijah to prepare people for his coming. God also said that when he came it would be like fire. Malachi 4 v 1 says, "The day is coming; it will burn like a furnace". No wonder Zechariah felt afraid! But in the following verse God added through Malachi, "But for you who revere [that is, love and respect] my name, the sun of righteousness will rise with healing in its rays."

In one sense, this prophecy came true when Jesus was born—that's when God came to earth. In another sense, it came true when Jesus died and rose again—that's when he made it possible for us to be healed and made righteous (or, made right with God). In another sense, we're still waiting for it to come true. One day Jesus will come back and the world as we know it will come to an end. But that's really a whole other story!

CHAPTER EIGHT

All the words the angel Gabriel speaks come directly from the Bible account. Have a look at Luke 1 v 26-38. What part of Gabriel's description of this impossible baby do you think is most exciting?

CHAPTER NINE

The story of when Samuel met Jesse's sons is told in 1 Samuel 16 v 1-13. In those days, kings didn't get crowned, they got anointed—that is, someone would pour oil on their forehead. That's what Samuel did to David. Even though at that point he wasn't actually king yet (and wouldn't rule Israel till years later), he was anointed with oil as a sign that God had chosen him.

CHAPTER TEN

Everything Elizabeth says to Mary in this chapter comes straight from the Bible account in Luke 1 v 39-45. The song Mary sings is also reported for us word for word in Luke 1 v 46-55. She must have been inspired by Hannah's song in 1 Samuel 2 v 1-10—there are a lot of similarities!

CHAPTER ELEVEN

Genesis 23 v 1-2 tells us that Sarah died at Hebron. Abraham bought a cave to bury her in (Genesis 23 v 17-20) and was later buried there himself by his son Isaac (Genesis 25 v 7-10). Later still, Isaac was buried there too (Genesis 35 v 27-29) and so was his son Jacob (Genesis 50 v 12-13). So this was a place with a lot of history! King Herod the Great built a large enclosure over the cave about 30 years before the birth of Jesus. The walls he built are still there even today.

The promise God made to Abraham about all the nations being blessed through his offspring is found in Genesis 22 v 18.

CHAPTER TWELVE

The book of Isaiah was written hundreds of years before Jesus was born. Matthew 1 v 22-23 points out that the bit of Isaiah that Zechariah is thinking about here (Isaiah 7 v 14) was predicting the events of the first Christmas, centuries later. The prophet Isaiah also predicted the fact that Jesus would suffer (in Isaiah 52 v 13 – 53 v 12). Zechariah wouldn't have known exactly what that meant—but now we know that God's plan involved Jesus dying on a cross in order to save all who trust in him.

CHAPTER THIRTEEN

Matthew 1 v 18-19 tells us about Joseph's plan not to marry Mary when he found out she was pregnant with a baby that was not his. It was a big deal to break off a betrothal—so big that Matthew actually calls it a "divorce", as if they were already married.

If you are eagle-eyed you might have noticed that Mary only stayed with Elizabeth for "about three months" (Luke 1 v 56)—so why does Joseph say that she's been away for three and a half? Well, we have to take into account travelling time: it would have been coming up for four months altogether. It's around that time that babies in the womb grow big enough to make their mother's baby bump begin to be noticeable.

CHAPTER FOURTEEN
Mary's story about the golden calf comes from Exodus 32 v 1-14. God did take the people's actions very seriously and punished them. In the end, though, he forgave them and promised once again to go with them into the promised land.

CHAPTER FIFTEEN
The Day of Trumpets is called Rosh Hashanah by Jewish people today: it's the Jewish New Year. Leviticus 23 v 23-25 and Numbers 29 v 1 contain God's instructions to the people about this festival.

We don't know exactly when John was born, but the Day of Trumpets seemed very appropriate to me! Read Luke 1 v 57-79 to find out what we do know for sure about John's birth.

CHAPTER SIXTEEN
The original tabernacle was built soon after God forgave his people for making the golden calf. The book of Exodus spends four whole chapters (35 – 38)

describing the building work! God told his people to celebrate the Feast of Tabernacles to remember the time they spent in the wilderness (Leviticus 23 v 39-43). It's still celebrated by Jewish people today—they call it Sukkot—and it takes place not long after the Day of Trumpets.

Read about Joseph's dream in Matthew 1 v 20-23. Matthew doesn't give us much detail, so I used my imagination a lot in this part of the story! But everything the angel says comes straight from the Bible account.

CHAPTER SEVENTEEN
Matthew 1 v 24 says, "When Joseph woke up, he did what the angel of the Lord had commanded him and took Mary home as his wife."

CHAPTER EIGHTEEN
The next few chapters tell the story of Luke 2 v 1-7.

Sepphoris—and Galilee more generally—really was a hotbed of rebels. Before Herod became king, he did a lot of fighting against Galilean bandits who were resisting the Romans. So the region would have had a bad name among those who were loyal to the king. After Herod's death in 4 BC—not long after the birth of Jesus—Sepphoris was the place where a rebel named Judas launched a major uprising.

We're so used to seeing pictures of Mary sitting on a donkey that I felt I had to include one—but in fact the

Bible doesn't actually mention one at all. People did use donkeys, but they were mostly pack-animals, carrying heavy loads so that their owners didn't have to. But Mary was heavily pregnant, so it's not unlikely that she would have sat on a donkey—as she will in the next chapter...

CHAPTER NINETEEN

We tend to think of Joseph and Mary going to Bethlehem completely on their own, but Joseph must have had family there. When I was writing this chapter, I enjoyed wondering why Joseph's family might not have wanted them to stay.

The book of Ruth tells us the story that Joseph refers to. Ruth was a Moabite, and generally speaking Moabites were the enemies of God's people. Ruth, though, decided to follow God and so she came to live in Bethlehem—but she was very poor and vulnerable. Boaz, an Israelite, admired her faith and married her. Now she was fully part of God's people, even though originally she hadn't been. Boaz and Ruth ultimately became the great-grandparents of King David.

CHAPTER TWENTY

Everyone assumes that Jesus was born in a stable—but that's not necessarily true. Luke simply tells us that Mary put Jesus in a manger (which just means a feeding trough). That does suggest that there were animals around—but people in the first century, especially poor ones like Gaddiel, often kept their animals inside their houses, not in separate stables! So the place described in this chapter is far more likely to have been the kind of place that Jesus was born in—a room that housed the animals.

CHAPTER TWENTY-ONE
Luke 2 v 8-20 tells us the story of the shepherds. I wonder whether you think I've got it right in the way I've imagined their reactions to the angels.

CHAPTER TWENTY-TWO
The book of Exodus tells the story of the first Passover: from the oppression of the Israelites (Exodus 1) to when Moses met God in a burning bush (3 v 1 – 4 v 17), through all the plagues God sent against the Egyptians (7 v 14 – 10 v 29) until finally God promised the death of all the firstborn sons, the people daubed their doorposts with lamb's blood and Pharaoh let them go at last (11 v 1 – 12 v 39). God told his people to eat this special meal of lamb not just once but again and again—every year—so they would never forget how he had rescued them.

When Zechariah and Elizabeth's son John met Jesus as an adult, he said, "Look, the Lamb of God, who takes away the sin of the world" (John 1 v 29). He was thinking of the Passover. The original lambs died in the place of the people's sons. Jesus died in the place of the whole world—taking all God's anger against sin upon himself, so that we could go free.

CHAPTER TWENTY-THREE

You can read the original account of Mary and Joseph's encounter with Simeon and Anna in Luke 2 v 22-38.

When Simeon said to Mary, "A sword will pierce your own soul too", he wasn't speaking literally. He was talking about the pain she would one day feel when she watched her son Jesus die on the cross. You can read that scene in John 19 v 16-30. Jesus was treated very brutally; it's not surprising that, as she watched, Mary felt like a sword was piercing her own soul.

CHAPTER TWENTY-FOUR

Have a look at Matthew 2 v 1-12 to see the Bible account of the visit of the wise men or "Magi". We don't know exactly where they came from, nor how many of them there were. It's actually possible that their visit didn't happen until Jesus was one or two years old—Matthew doesn't give us a date. But it could equally have taken place fairly soon after Jesus was born, as it does here.

CHAPTER TWENTY-FIVE

Matthew 2 v 13-18 tells us about Joseph's dream and the escape to Egypt. It's possible that they didn't spend long in Egypt at all—Matthew 2 v 19-21 tells us that they came back when King Herod died, which may have been soon after Jesus was born. (They might even have gone after the birth and returned before the visit to the temple—but I chose to put the temple visit first.)

Acknowledgements

It's amazing that this book got written, because I had injured hands while I wrote it. So I'm very grateful: first to God, of course, and second to the many people who supported me as I wrote. In particular, thanks are due to...

My editors, Alison and Carl: your encouragement, wisdom and enthusiasm kept me going and made the book better than I could have made it on my own. Also André, Lex and all my other colleagues at The Good Book Company. I am very grateful for you.

Chris Morphew and Professor Steve Mason, for your helpful input at the beginning and end of the writing process.

Rachel and Anna for cooking me meals, driving me around, building me desks, making me laugh, giving me hugs and generally being excellent companions in what really was a very strange time.

My parents, who started me off, both with writing and with God. Thank you for teaching me, caring for me, inspiring me, and showing me what it means to love the Lord. I hope this book has something of you both in it.

thegoodbook
COMPANY

BIBLICAL | RELEVANT | ACCESSIBLE

At The Good Book Company, we are dedicated to helping Christians and local churches grow. We believe that God's growth process always starts with hearing clearly what he has said to us through his timeless word—the Bible.

Ever since we opened our doors in 1991, we have been striving to produce Bible-based resources that bring glory to God. We have grown to become an international provider of user-friendly resources to the Christian community, with believers of all backgrounds and denominations using our books, Bible studies, devotionals, evangelistic resources, and DVD-based courses.

We want to equip ordinary Christians to live for Christ day by day, and churches to grow in their knowledge of God, their love for one another, and the effectiveness of their outreach.

Call us for a discussion of your needs or visit one of our local websites for more information on the resources and services we provide.

Your friends at The Good Book Company

thegoodbook.com | thegoodbook.co.uk
thegoodbook.com.au | thegoodbook.co.nz
thegoodbook.co.in